Raindrops from dreams

OrangeBooks Publication

Smriti Nagar, Bhilai, Chhattisgarh - 490020

Website: **www.orangebooks.in**

© Copyright, 2022, Author

All rights reserved. No part of this book may be reproduced, stored in a retrieval system, or transmitted, in any form by any means, electronic, mechanical, magnetic, optical, chemical, manual, photocopying, recording or otherwise, without the prior written consent of its writer.

First Edition, 2022

Dinesh Kumar R S

OrangeBooks Publication
www.orangebooks.in

Dedicated to my better half, and my better sum

Also, my heartfelt thanks to my mother

PREFACE

These are some of my dreams, nine out of many, that refused to fade from my mind the next day, and even started gnawing my thoughts like a stubborn baby suckling its mama's tits. They pestered me until I meticulously wrote them in a piece of paper (whatever I could remember or could make sense of) so that I could elaborate and write it as a story for others to read.

The common theme in all my stories is pain and the raindrops.

Imagine yourself suffering with pain that is devouring both your body and mind standing in the middle of a desert and suddenly a couple of the coolest raindrops fall on your face announcing the arrival of a downpour later. What would be your reaction? At least for a couple of seconds, it may take away your pain and that little time may work wonders in your life, may change your perspective or may lift your spirits higher than ever.

You may ask if all my dreams are about pain since all my stories deal with it. My answer would be the following.

All living things fear pain and go to great extent to escape from it. Human race is no exception since we would even sell our souls to avoid pain as much as possible. But if we look through the pages of our past, we can understand that pain and suffering had a greater role to play than given credit for in shaping our civilization. The need to escape from pain triggered our brain to find solutions faster and we evolved quicker than our fellow bipeds. Does it mean there is no divine intervention? Did we survive the countless perils we faced only with our intelligent brain? I do not think so.

There is an inconceivable, unimaginable, immeasurable, unquantifiable, illogical, nonsensical, incomprehensible, inexplicable force that affects our every action. Some may call this imaginary force as 'God,' some may call this as 'Gaia,' some may call it as the "Force" as in 'May the force be with you' while most would not even consider to give it a name and instead focus on finding answers based on scientific theologies.

In these stories you may think of the raindrops as the imaginary force because it is a catalyst that alleviates or exacerbates pain suffered by the characters in the stories depending on their roles. Atheists may not view this as divine intervention and the theists may not believe that there is a scientific explanation.

So dear readers, if you are an atheist or an agnostic do not worry because I have not talked about any religion in these stories. It is just a collection of raindrops that fall unexpectedly on the characters and would make them self-aware, or repent, or embolden, or ruminate, or feel content, or bittersweet, or baffled or besotted.

Dear readers, I am sure that after reading all the stories, you would also experience an ambivalent set of emotions and you may also try to find any logic or reason for all the happenings in the stories. However, my only intent is to just ruffle your sense of morality.

Dinesh Kumar

Raindrops are my only remainder that clouds have a heartbeat.

That I have one too.

Tahereh Mafi

RAINDROP 1

We are near waking when we dream, we are dreaming

Novalis

The Chinese ghost and the sea snake

Pain, pain and, more pain.

It hurt like hell; the pain spread throughout my body like a fire monster devouring everything it touched wreaking havoc to anything in its path. I could see flashing lights and vibrant colors like I was in a psychedelic dream world. I wondered how I got here in the first place and more importantly how to get out. It is time I woke up from this dreadful place where the only feeling I could experience was pain except I cannot feel anything else not even my body, not even the usual itch behind my ears or the moistness on my palms even during the coldest night. As I pondered over this unimaginable imaginary situation, the fire monster resumed its cataclysmic journey through my imaginary body.

Suddenly I was floating in the air, suspended above the clouds. I saw a bright light in the distant horizon which I assumed was the sun but it could not be because the glowing orb seemed to radiate a kaleidoscopic ray of light. Even though it shone brightly, I could see the multicolored sun without squinting. After watching it for a long time, I saw the clouds like soft pillows. At last, I am in heaven. Adios to you, you blasted fire monster. I was relieved that I felt no more pain.

I could feel a soft breeze gently caressing me. Instinctively I scratched my ears and felt my face with my hands and the wrinkles on my forehead. Does it mean, I am not dead. I saw that my body was intact and except for the irritation in my eyes as the soft breeze had turned into a gale, I was doing fine. I felt tired. My eyes were begging to close and I strained to see that I was slowly descending into the clouds. I could feel the chillness of the clouds as I passed them on my way down. In heaven, the clouds were resting place for the tired souls. Now I was descending rapidly and soon I realized that I was dropping like a stone.

I could see the big blue ocean below with no boundaries. I was now falling like a meteorite.

Where would I land? No. Where would I crash?

I had a crazy idea. I wanted to see my body hitting the ground. Maybe my body would explode on impact not like a bomb blast throwing its shrapnel everywhere but more like a decayed, gaseous blob hitting the ground at great speed spewing rotten bits of flesh all around. Or it would stick to the ground like chewing gum on the street trampled on by thousands of feet or it would just break into a thousand pieces like the sudden dispersion of a school of fish when threatened by a predator.

I could see no more as darkness enveloped me and I could not help falling asleep. Even though I slept, I could feel the gravity accelerating my body's descent.

I woke up or was I waken.

The bright multicolored sun overhead made me squint my eyes.

Where was I?

I was lying in the sand, soft and white as cotton on a small island in the middle of an ocean.

How did I come here? I wondered. I remembered that I was in pain, and by some miracle it was gone. I could feel my body again which meant that I was not dead. I was falling from a great height. And the fall would have killed me instantly, but I was alive. Scratching my ears, I looked around at the tiny parcel of land.

The island was a miracle. It was ridiculously small. A small dot of white in a large portrait filled with blue. It was no more than 400 square feet. In the center of the circular island was the tallest coconut tree that I had ever seen in my life. Its narrow trunk extending more than 500 feet in the air. It was so tall that I could hardly see the coconuts. Maybe there was none.

My throat was parched and I yearned for a drop of water. I was in the middle of quadrillion liters of water maybe more but couldn't quench my thirst. Something landed near my feet with a big thud. My heart skipped a beat as I jumped in surprise. I laughed aloud when I found the thing that scared me shitless.

It was a small coconut lying half-buried in the ground. I found a sharp sea shell and started to chip away the hard shell. I punctured a small hole and drank heartily. It was the sweetest thing that I ever tasted. I could feel the cool water washing my throat, and fill my stomach. I was refreshed and my spirit soared high. My stomach grumbled at me like a dog baring its teeth. I ate the soft flesh inside the coconut and felt the iron grip of hunger slowly relax.

Small, white waves crashed against the island in perfect rhythm and in the distance, I could see dolphins jump out of the water. I strained my eyes to spot any distant speck of land but all I saw was the blue ocean on every side. I felt like a shipwrecked sailor except that my arrival was still a mystery. The day progressed very slowly as I watched the shadow of the tree move as the sun like sphere travelled across the sky. I yearned for some company as I spent the rest of the day thinking hard about the different scenarios that I may face.

What would a big wave do to this little parcel of land just a few feet higher than the gigantic ocean? I was sure that this piece of land would sink into the big blue along with me. Maybe I could climb the tree and save myself. But what to do if it happened when I was asleep. I didn't know what to do except stare at the blue water, the white waves, the blue sky, the multicolored sun, and of course the tall coconut tree. It was getting cold as the sun like sphere began to set in the western horizon.

I was again hungry and looked up at the tree wishing for another coconut. But this time, nothing happened. I tried to climb the tree but it proved more difficult than I thought. I could climb no higher than five feet and slid down to the ground. The tree was too smooth, I reckoned.

Maybe I could take a dip in the water.

I removed my clothes and was about to step into the water, when a long sea snake, golden with bold blue bands swam towards me. I instantly retreated to safety. The sea snake was almost eleven feet in length and venomous. I looked with fear at the snake swimming around the island. My fear turned to awe as I noted its beauty. Its body was shimmering in the evening sun and it seemed to glide gracefully in the clear water. I waited for it to leave.

After a long time, I saw it swim away and disappear. I ought to be more careful in the future. I again stepped nimbly into the water, without disturbing the sand in the bottom. I could see some oysters and some crabs and tried to grab some when I again saw the sea snake in the corner of my eyes swimming towards me.

I hastily stepped out of the water as it nearly bit me. I could see it was very pissed at me and it showed its fangs and flicked its tongue. It swam near the island for a longer time and finally disappeared below.

I saw the orange disk of the sun slipping into the water. The big blue ocean had gobbled the sun. It was getting dark now. Panic gripped me again. Reality slapped my face hard. I could not start a fire. I didn't know whether the ocean would gobble me too. I didn't know if sea snakes could slide on land. And I couldn't climb the damn tree.

It became darker till I could see no more. I sat near the tree, hugging it tightly with my eyes closed with fear. Somehow, I mustered enough courage to open my eyes after some time. My eyes adjusted and saw a whole new world in the night. I could see the water shimmering. The bright neon blue haze of the water was breathtaking. I had heard of bioluminescent algae in the water but had never seen one.

Dolphins jumped out of the water and dropped down into the ocean. I could see that they too glowed. I could see schools of fish swimming near the island eating the seaweeds growing in the shallow water; I could see phosphorescent corals teeming with glowing creatures.

As I stepped near the water taking in the marvelous sights, my friend reappeared as I saw that it too glowed. Its blue bands now glowed with a brilliant electric blue hue. I went back to my place near the coconut tree. Slowly my eyelids closed and sleep overtook me.

I didn't know how long I slept and it was still night. Feeling a slight movement, I looked up at the tree and almost screamed when I saw a figure watching me from the tree. I felt my heart pounding in my chest, and I trembled with fear.

Run, my mind commanded but my body ceased to listen and stood like a rock.

Even if ran, I would not get far on that tiny island. Maybe I could swim away but the thought of the sea snake and other unimaginable dangers hiding in the deep stopped me.

Slowly the figure climbed down. Now I could see her. She was Asian and wore a blue silk knee-length cheongsam that hugged her body. I could see her gracious curves and found that she was gifted in abundance with everything in its place.

She walked towards me, slowly and steadily like a predator stalking its prey, her hips gently swaying, and her two eyes looking angrily at me like raised swords. Her face was pale and her lips were blue like a corpse.

Fear gripped me again and the word 'Ghost' flashed red in my mind.

She came near me till her breasts almost touched my chest and looked deep into my eyes. She parted her bow-shaped lips, glistening in the blue light. Her moist tongue darted out and ran over her mouth. I felt a new sensation tingling down my spine.

I don't know which I felt more. Fear or pleasure?

Should I take the red pill or the blue pill.

Should I swim through the trench or over it.

She is definitely a ghost., I thought. A Chinese ghost judging from her dress.

She smiled and my heart which was trying to get out a few minutes back melted at her girlish beauty. She was a young girl who was not destined to die early and could have lived few more years. I swore angrily at God for plucking such a beautiful fruit at such a tender age.

It died but not decayed as I could see it was ravishing even after death. The girl watched me in amusement as a myriad of thoughts most of them unclean raced through my mind. I couldn't control myself any longer.

I hugged her tightly and was relieved when she hugged me back. I closed my eyes tightly and my mouth found its way to hers. I could feel her tongue delve deep inside mine trying to get deeper swirling inside my throat. Pulling away from my grasp, she stepped back and removed her clothes till she was naked.

I had judged correctly. She was perfect.

She watched me seductively with eyebrows bent like a bow and her piercing black eyes that looked through me. Her slender neck ended in a chest that was home to two beautiful melons.

She had a perfect pair of breasts. Not small and not big. It was standing erect like a lamp post. Perky and pointed with baby pink nipples. It jiggled at the slightest movement. She was narrow in the middle and her body enlarged to form beautiful hips. I could not see her behind but guessed that it would be as beautiful as the front. A dark bush grew between her legs, hiding her secret- another pair of lips hid behind.

She let me examine her body with a teasing smirk.

I sprang into action and felt that I should not waste any more time lest she disappears. I hugged her again and felt her pointy things pricking me. I kissed her deeply; my hands went behind her and measured her lovely bumps in the back.

I slowly laid her on the ground and watched her look at me with a sly grin. I quickly ditched my clothes and crawled towards her like a toddler. My mouth instinctively went for her lips- the other lips waiting for me behind the bush. As I parted them with my mouth and sucked them, she slowly kissed her way down my waist with a purpose till a part of my body was sucked in by a moist vacuum and saw it disappear inside her mouth. Then it was time for the grand finale.

I laid on top of her, once again our tongues danced like snakes and she guided me to my destination. I pushed my body firmly and felt it get sucked into a deep crevasse. She moaned loudly as I showed her the tricks that I had learned in my life. I was in the seventh heaven when I climaxed and slept with my now flaccid tool still inside her body.

I woke the next morning to find her gone.

A single coconut fell and again satisfied my hunger. My slithery friend showed again near the shore and swam around the island and tried to bite every time I went near the water. I spent the rest of the day in misery and hoped that the Chinese ghost would come again. I watched the tree's shadow move till it completely disappeared and the day gave in to night as the stars shone brightly in the sky.

The Chinese ghost didn't disappoint me. She appeared as usual and we rolled over the sand hugging each other.

I slept again after a wonderful time and woke up the next morning to find her gone as usual.

This drama went on for many days. The story was the same with some minor changes. Only the positions changed. Sometimes I had sex with her back against the tree. Sometimes she sat on top of me, her tits jiggling till I was spent. Sometimes she kneeled as I came at her from behind. Sometimes we just cuddled together, our bodies entangled in a tight embrace, and watched the stars blinking in the vast sky.

All good things come to an end.

It came one fine day and I was the one who was the cause of it.

One night while I was making love to her, I blurted my undying romance to her and begged her not to leave me again. I could not stand being lonely the next day and had to bear the long wait yearning for her till midnight. I threatened to kill myself by slipping into the ocean if she left me.

Her eyes blazed with anger and her nostrils flared throwing fiery breaths at my face. She opened her mouth and sank her teeth into my flesh. I screamed with pain as my eyes blurred. I saw her getting dimmer as her body slowly transformed into a sea snake and slid into the water. I could not wonder whether her true form was the snake or a beautiful girl.

I lay on the sand scolding myself when the first of the raindrops fell on my face. It soon started to rain heavily and washed the tears from my face. I welcomed the coolness spreading over my body. I didn't know when I slept, thinking whether she would come back the next day or the day after or whether I will see her again.

I slowly opened my eyes to welcome the next day with high hopes. My eyelids felt like rocks as I felt something pulsating in my head till I realized that it was my long-lost friend announcing its return. A dull throbbing pain soon shot through my body, as the fire monster once again continued its journey devouring my flesh. My vision was blurred as I looked around and soon it became clear as I took note of the periphery. My brain tried to make sense of the images relayed by my eyes.

I was lying on a hard bed; my head was bandaged and some machines were beeping next to me. I looked around and saw a nurse absent-mindedly enter the room with some files. She dropped them as she caught my attention, gasped loudly, and fled.

I could hear her feet scampering away and soon I heard more feet running towards me. She returned with more nurses who looked at me in bewilderment. Two doctors entered the room and they too looked at me in shock.

Finally, I heard one of the doctors speak...

I can't believe my eyes; he told the other doctor. His brain functions started to weaken each day and I thought he would be brain dead very soon. I even asked his family to opt to pull the plug. In my twenty years of experience, I had never seen a patient recovering from a coma after suffering such a heavy trauma to the head. He must be a lucky bastard.

Someone was watching over him, the other doctor said and he didn't allow him to die.

My memories returned to me as I recalled the truck crashing against my car and my head hitting the dashboard. The last thing that entered my mind before I lost consciousness was that I would die.

As I lay on the bed, staring at the picture of a tropical island at the far end of the wall, I realized that I was lost in a dream. I dreamt of an island in the middle of an ocean.

I realized that my mind was the tiny island in the ocean.

And the Chinese ghost and the sea snake kept my mind active

Whenever my mind felt like sinking into the blue water, my friend the sea snake prevented me from doing so and when I felt lonely, the Chinese ghost held me close.

It was they who saved me and the raindrops.

RAINDROP 2

Too many of us are not living our dreams because we are living our fears.

Les Brown

Knight of the night

The stone-faced man was driving a shiny black Mercedes slowly in the night streets of New Delhi, his eyes piercing through the smog that hung like a veil covering the face of a newly married bride waiting anxiously for her husband on her first night.

He was searching for something in the almost empty streets and nothing escaped him.as he watched carefully for anything that moved in the shadows, taking his time to examine every nook and cranny.

It was 3 A.M.

The streets were deserted except for some street urchins loitering near the dump bins looking for any leftovers, some poor souls sleeping on the sidewalks wrapped in crude rags, huddled together for some warmth against the bitter cold of December night and stray dogs chasing a lone bitch trying to escape from their frenzy.

The car circled Rajiv Chowk Park and turned towards radial road 5. It then reached the wider Connaught circle road.

The man was still searching the vacant roads and his eyes widened when he saw some youngsters walking on the road after partying at one of the pubs. He slowed his car as he scanned them with interest, and after some deep thought he moved on. The car then moved on to the next stop at Chanakyapuri and prowled near the clubs where some groups were still partying on the streets. He again slowed down the car and his eagle eyes pierced at them like a predator eyeing its prey.

After some time, he again moved on and ignored the cries of the teenagers with beer cans asking him for a ride.

A police patrol car came to view and the man quickly turned the car into a narrow street. He watched the youngsters dispersing after the police officers warned them for creating a public nuisance.

After chasing the youngsters away, the patrol car proceeded on its usual route.

The man watching the now-empty street clenched his fists and punched the dashboard in frustration. He could not find what he was searching for. Maybe tomorrow, he said loudly and turned the car towards the main road. The car was accelerating when the man hit the brakes. It screeched to a halt in the middle of the road as the headlights illuminated a young girl standing a few feet away looking bewildered at the car.

A smile crept slowly into the man's face and soon turned to a grin when he scanned the girl.

She was beautiful in her early twenties wearing a black low-neck top showing ample cleavage and stopped above her navel. A black mini skirt started well below her waist exposed her long legs.

She came near the car and tapped at the window.

Sir, she called like a lost puppy.

The man rolled down the window and glanced at her.

My friends ditched me when the police arrived. I have lost my phone and couldn't contact them. I don't want to spend the night in the streets. Could you drop me at this address?

The girl was close to tears as she told him the directions to her place.

The man smiled and nodded. Anything for the damsel in distress, he replied and signaled to get inside the car.

She walked unsteadily to the other side and got inside the car.

I drank one too many, she laughed as she spoke. The stench of alcohol dissipated from the girl's mouth and filled the car. The man rolled down his windows and took a deep breath.

The girl turned on the dome lights and looked at the mirror in the sun visor, examining her makeup.

Women he thought.

Could you please turn off the light? It is distracting me he said.

The light didn't affect his driving.

He didn't want her to see his face, his devilish grin spread from ear to ear and the saliva forming in the corners of his mouth. He decided to put his plan into motion.

I don't think we could make the trip to your place as the car is low on fuel, he lied. Why don't you come to my place for the night, take rest he said. I promise that I will drop you at daybreak.

She didn't answer.

Miss, can you hear me.

After a long time, she replied.

Yes, but I don't want to be a burden to your family.

Don't worry about that, he replied. I will take care of you.

The car now was speeding towards the man's house.

It entered a posh neighborhood where the rich and famous lived-in pomp and luxury. Beautiful bungalows with well-maintained gardens were visible on either side of the road, bordered by butea monosperma trees and a walking track running parallel to the road intersected with benches.

Wow, said the girl looking at the houses illuminated bright as day. I really envy you rich folk and your lifestyle. It's like I have entered a part of India vastly different from the rest.

The car halted before the gates of a beautiful bungalow and the gates opened automatically allowing the car to enter.

The man parked the car and opened the door for the girl to step out.

A gentleman indeed she cried. I feel safer already.

Welcome to Faraway Boulevard proclaimed the man where your worries would go far away from you.

A poet too, the girl laughed mischievously and bit her lips. Is that so? She said running her fingers over her cleavage.

The man opened the front door and let her inside the house. Dim lights switched on automatically and music played somewhere.

The man pointed at the bar. Mahogany shelves containing expensive liquor bottles welcomed the guests. Oak round tables with focus lights and bar chairs were placed around them.

She graciously accepted his invitation, went to the bar, and selected a bottle of scotch.

The glasses are inside the lower shelf and the ice cubes are in the fridge. The man showed her their locations.

Can you pour me a glass, love?

Sure, the girl answered and took out two glasses.

How many ice cubes? she asked him.

Two the man replied.

She poured the whiskey into the glasses and added the ice cubes.

The man was sitting on a sofa at the far end of the room watching the news on the flat TV placed on the wall. He watched her from the corner of his eye cat walking towards him seductively. She stumbled on the way and almost dropped the drinks.

I almost fell, she cried. Don't you have any bright lights in the house?

I am allergic to bright lights whispered the man. I like to live in the shadows.

The man took the drink from her and clinked against her glass.

Cheers, she said and started to sip the drink. This is some good stuff, she nodded with appreciation. She finished the drink, went for another round, and came back after refilling her glass.

I like this place very much she shouted. She went back to refill three more times.

After some time, she climbed on the round table and started to dance like a swinger. I feel horny she said as she removed her tops.

He could see the silhouette of her body in the dim lights. She pushed her skirt down and threw it away.

The girl kneeled and shouted.

Now I am your slave, master and your wish are my command.

She watched him looking at her with a gaping mouth.

Do you want to fuck?

Only if you scream, he replied. She screamed with excitement at the top of her voice.

Only out of fear he continued. You see I am like the Knight in medieval times. I get turned on only if I see a damsel in distress.

He diverted her attention to the TV.

The headlines screamed the news of a serial killer who was wreaking havoc for the past year. Mutilated bodies of young girls were found dumped in the sewage and so far, eight bodies were found in various stages of decay.

He shook his head in frustration.

What incompetent nincompoops are they? He grumbled angrily. The police had only found eight of the sixteen bodies.

The girl was looking at him and he saw that she was shaking with fear.

Did you kill the girls? The girl whispered.

Yes, he said beaming with pride. I killed all sixteen of them. And the number will be seventeen by tomorrow.

I still remember my first kill. She was a homeless woman in her late twenties and reeked of the slums. She was overjoyed when I let her inside my house and ran down the hallway like a giddy school girl. As she happily explored my house, I was thinking of a dozen ways to torture her, to stop her smiling and fill her face with dread.

Should I puncture her freckled face with needles and watch a thousand trickles of blood forming on her face or should I just slit her throat to stop her from chattering endlessly.

I still remember the blood gashing out when I slit her throat. I killed her too soon. Then I started slicing her body with the butcher knife. It was a total mess.

My first kill was out of blind hatred. My anger subsided after that and I started killing my next victims with more panache.

I am not a person who would go after any girl because I am a man with specific tastes. Only the beautiful and young girls are lucky enough to interest me and so I started to search for them in the streets of Delhi often searching for hours, and return home empty handed on most nights.

I bring the lucky ones here and watch their body turn numb after intaking their spiked drinks.

I remove their clothes and lay them naked o the table. As they watch me with their fearful eyes, I slowly slice their bodies making thin incisions with a surgical knife. I then gouge their eyes, slice their tongues and if the girl is still alive, I will slice her nipples. I climax when their pupils dilate and their pathetic souls leave their bodies.

Then the actual mutilations start and by the time I finish, their bodies would be in pieces.

Sometimes I do little experiments with them.

Like what would happen if I pour boiling water directly in their noses through a funnel or what would happen if I place a red-hot iron ball on their belly buttons.

He came out of his trance.

You must wonder why I am doing this. It is because slicing and dicing young vixens like you is more enjoyable than sex.

You have managed to not cry till now and have disappointed me so far by not giving me the pleasure of hearing your pathetic attempt to beg for your life. It's time you faced your worst nightmare.

Lightning flashed outside followed by thunder rumbling in the night sky. It started to rain heavily.

He looked at the girl still kneeling on the table like a statue. Suddenly a bright flash irradiated the room followed by a crashing thunder that deafened the ears. I have activated the security systems and all the doors are locked. You can't escape from me, little girl.

He guffawed like the villain in old western movies.

The power failed and the house was thrown into darkness.

He turned on his mobile. The room was pitch dark and the tiny light from his mobile phone threw faint light which he used to scan the room. The house was silent as the grave as he searched for the girl.

Darkness and Silence are adversaries working together since ancient times creating ghastly images in the human mind and driving them to the path of desperation and madness. It is no surprise that humans believe that the worst embodiments of evil come out in the middle of the night to devour them.

The girl was nowhere. He could no longer bear the absence of sound as he focused his extremely sensitive ears to detect even tiny sounds that escape most humans. He wished that he could hear the girl's breathing under the table or the sound of her sweat dripping on the floor or the faint scrapping on the floor when she shifted her position.

Nothing. All he could hear was silence.

He didn't expect this new turn of events as he strained to find the girl. Usually, they would scream at the top of their voice and try to escape from him or they would freeze like a statue like a possum playing dead when threatened. Time seemed to stand still, as he felt tiny beads of perspiration pricking his body and he could hear the sound of drums and realized that it was his heart beat. He was experiencing something which he never felt before. It was not the thrill he felt when he hunted the girls in the darkest nights. He finally understood the feeling but it was hard to accept.

It was fear.

The fear of the unknown grasps the human mind so tightly that it ceases to function and abandons all logic. To overcome this terror, the stone-faced man tried to assert that he was still in control of the situation.

Maybe she ran to the other rooms, he thought as he turned a full circle. Sensing that she was not in the Living room, he decided to move to the next room. He meticulously searched the other rooms, the bedrooms on the first floor, the kitchen, the library, the attic, the terrace, the bathrooms and the even the garden within the compound, but he couldn't find any trace of the girl.

Filled with disappointment he again entered the house and concluded that she somehow managed to give him the slip when the power failed. He removed his wet clothes and changed into his night robe. He shuddered as the music system came alive and the lights turned on. He wondered what had affected his nerves of steel so that he jumped at the even the slightest sounds. Pouring himself a large whiskey, he checked the CCTVs that he had installed in his house to find how the girl had escaped.

As he searched through the footage, he found an oddity in the image shown by one of the cameras. It showed the trapdoor which was always locked except on special occasions that led to the basement where he had setup his entertainment room- the place where he did his experiments on his prey.

The trapdoor was open exposing a dark abyss.

He again laughed loudly. I found you, bitch and you can't escape my clutches. With renewed energy he ran to the trapdoor and descended the staircase till he felt the cold floor of the basement. The lights turned on automatically sensing his presence and he scanned the room. A surgical bed was present in the center of the room and various instruments that can cut the flesh, grind the bones, puncture the skull were kept near the bed for easy access. Various parts of the human body, the eyes, ears, brain, and other organs were displayed in glass cupboards illuminated brightly. The man looked at the room with pride and again resumed his search for the missing girl behind the cupboards, behind the sofa, under the sink till he heard the screeching sounds from the bathroom.

Moving like a cat, he tiptoed across the room, turned the handle softly and entered the bathroom. Turning on the light he saw the silhouette of a person behind the shower curtain.

With a devilish grin, he said loudly.

I can see your lips quivering and your body shaking with fear, however a shimmer of hope that you can escae from this house still festers somewhere in your mind.

But you also know that it is a futile thought, so I will clear your doubts right now. You can't escape from me now. Before you die, you deserve to know that you had given me the most electrifying experience and I am grateful for that. I will make sure that I will be highly creative when torturing you.

A loud crash followed by continuing rumbling indicated the lightening had struck near the house and again darkness engulfed the house. Turning on his mobile phone's torch he focused the light on the shower curtain when he sensed a movement from behind.

He felt the hair on his neck raise when something cold as ice pressed against his back.

Can you escape me?

An unnatural voice like an animal sounded from behind.

He turned the light slowly till it shone on the mirror on the wall, reflecting his face at the edge of panic and suddenly the girl's pale face devoid of emotions peeked over his shoulders, her eyes glowing red in the dark and the smell of death emanating from her.

Can you escape death? The voice asked him again. You said that you can recall all your victims, but do you want to see them again, the voice continued.

Her face changed rapidly into the faces of his victims. The face of his first kills appeared, then the face of his next kill and the next, and so on. The faces continued to change.

You like to live in the shadows but my home is the darkness.

He screamed as he had never screamed before. With a sudden burst of energy, he ran towards the staircase, quickly climbed it, and closed the trapdoor. Before he could lock the trapdoor, it burst open. Screaming loudly, he ran towards the front door never looking back. Exiting the house, he ran towards the gate across the lawn when a hand-pulled his leg making him fall heavily on the wet lawn.

He was sprawled face down on the ground and felt the wet grass in his mouth. He felt a strong pair of hands turning him till he faced the girl.

The girl sat on his chest and laughed at him. Lightning streaked across the night sky and blinded him for an instant.

Do you think the tormented souls of your victims would not take revenge? Have you experienced real agony and wished that you were never born? Have you ever waited anxiously for death to come knocking at your door? Let me introduce you to the world of pain. Listen carefully for you have only a couple of minutes before you will lose your hearing and other senses.

I have known pain since the day I was born. I barely survived when my parents tried to poison me the day I was born, when I was just taking in the first of my breaths, because they were expecting a boy. I should have died that day since death would have freed me but fate intervened. My mother never touched me because she thought that I brought bad luck to the house and my father looked at me like I was the harbinger of death.

I passed my time, counting the scars on my body, from my father's whip, and licked the fresh wounds from the previous night. As I grew, I watched my little brother born a year after me treated like a king. He was given delicious foods, played with fancy toys and wore beautiful dresses while I ate the leftovers, and punished for breathing the same air as him. Noone in my village looked at me and no one cared for me. When sickness spread through my village, many succumbed to it included my brother. I watched my parents wailing over the pale lifeless body of my brother. Soon after my brother's demise, my mother set fire to herself. I watched the flames engulf her body as she ran around the hut screaming like a banshee.

My father cursed and blamed me for the successive calamities and regretted for not throwing me into the well the day I was born. I prayed to God to kill me, burn my body, and erase me from existence. I was barely nine years and probably the only kid who was very earnest to die. But my pain didn't end and only escalated in the coming days.

I was grabbed by three strangers in the middle of the night and felt something thrust inside my mouth so I couldn't scream. I cried loudly but my screams were barely audible to me lest it could be heard by others and I was stuffed inside a sack I saw my father's angry face looking at me with disgust from the far end of the hut.

He spat when I scooped my hands to beg him to come to my rescue.

I thrashed with all my strength and struggled to escape from my captors but only received a rally of blows all over my body. I had never experienced such grueling pain before and thought that I would die. I lost consciousness when something crashed against my head.

I woke up in a strange place dimly lit with oil lamps and felt sharp pangs of pain in my head. I looked around and saw a huge statue of a woman dressed in a red sari looking fiercely at me with a long tongue dangling from her blood red mouth. She looked like the statue of the village Goddess which was carried on a bullock cart on festive days through the village, people following in procession singing and dancing in ecstasy felt that my prayers were finally answered and I would soon find solace in her bosom. I realized in the next instant, how foolish I had been when a hand ripped off my clothes till, I wore nothing except my skin. Then the stranger pounced on me like a giant snake smothering a tiny lamb. The beast started to bite all over my body as I felt his teeth sink deeply into my flesh.

I felt a burning sensation between my legs and felt the pain increasing exponentially as the beast rocked its body. After inflicting much pain, the beast left and was replaced by another. The pain continued till I felt no more.

I envied the lamb struggling under the coils of the giant snake because at least its pain would vanish as soon as its life slipped from its body. I slipped in and out of consciousness as the beasts ripped my body day and night till I lost count. I watched the angry eyes of the Goddess still glaring at me. Was she disgusted with looking at me daily or was she blaming me for defiling her sacred sanctuary? Maybe she was angry with the beasts that tormented me or was she frustrated that she was unable to do anything. She was after all made of stone.

The beasts finally grew tired of me and decided to finally grant me the death that eluded me for long. On a dark moonless night, I was laid on the bullock cart which usually carried the Goddess and my journey continued as the cart slowly rolled over uneven ground to an unknown destination.

When I woke up, I felt a strong wind blowing over me and poking at the many wounds on my body. I was hanging upside down and one of my legs was caught in the branches of a tree growing on the steep slope of a mountain overlooking a deep gorge. The beasts must have thrown me off the mountain thinking that I would plunge to my death but how mistaken they were. Why should I give them the satisfaction of deciding my death, I thought and slowly tried to dislodge my leg.

Then I saw the shadows dangling on the branches of the tree moaning and wailing loudly. I understood that they were trying to communicate with me and soon it began to make sense when I listened. I felt their pain and desolation as they howled loudly about the misfortunes of their past. I listened to their stories as I clung to the tree tightly, so that I could prolong my existence. It became clear that my pain was nothing compared to theirs and I was fighting to stay alive a little longer, till I heard all their stories. Maybe the Goddess would at least grant me this wish. My eyes filled with tears as they narrated their past and even in my pathetic situation, I could not help but feel sorry for them. There was nothing that I could do to ease their suffering and watched the shadows dancing around me.

What should I do, I cried. What can I do?

I cried in exasperation

Survive, they shouted in unison. Fight hard and survive

I have no strength, I cried. The beasts devoured my body and I am rotting from the inside. Let me join you after I die, so at least after death, I am not alone.

No, they cried. We will not let you die. Let us help you. You need not be alive but neither should you die.

My body become light and the pain seemed to slowly fade like the morning mist disappear when the sun rises. Maybe my soul had left its mortal shell and was ascending towards the great beyond. Suddenly I was caught in a whirlpool and felt immense pressure in my chest.

You are not alone, the voices cried. We have become one and now our journey will continue.

I became a ghoul neither alive nor dead as they entered my body.

The girl looked at the man with a devilish glow in her eyes.

It has been days since I had a decent meal, she whispered and I will make sure that I eat your flesh slowly. Who knows when I may taste such a delicious food again.

And now I want you to scream really loud this time. You will experience the pain of the girls when they were defiled by you and I will not let you die till I have sucked every drop of blood from your body, feasted on every bit of flesh sticking to your bones, chewed every bone in your body and sucked the marrow from the bones till my appetite is sated.

She sank her teeth into his body, biting and tearing large chunks of flesh.

He continued to scream as the rain fell on his body.

But it had stopped raining a long time ago. It was his blood that splattered everywhere.

RAINDROP 3

No person has the right to rain on your dreams.

Marian Wright Edelman

The Nutcracker

A large crowd waited before the family courtroom No.5 chatting casually about the weather, the latest gossips about celebrities, and some other trivial things happening in the city. Most of them were young women, some of them waited alone while others waited with an elderly gent or a lady. Some of the men were looking at the women with hatred in their eyes and their once beloveds tried to avert their eyes to something else. Some of the people were engrossed in their mobile phones, stood like statues except for their hands which were constantly flicking, the touchscreens of the mobile phones. Lawyers entered the courtroom with a big bundle of papers and settled themselves comfortably in the chairs placed before a raised dais where the judge sat in his high chair. Noone was permitted inside the courtroom except the legal practitioners till their names were announced by the judge's attendant.

It was easy to separate the newcomers and the veterans. Anyone could tell the difference by watching their eyes, the mirrors of the human souls. The newcomers were the restless ones, their eyes constantly scanning the room with anxiety and stealing glances at their partners while the people who waited alone, staring with cold indifference were the veterans whose case was still awaiting judgment for many years. The people who stood as a group, chatting excitedly were the chaperones who were accustomed to the routine. The newcomers waited with high hopes, the chaperones tried to make the best of their time while the veterans just persisted.

Everyone was waiting for the judge's arrival. Lawyers were lecturing their clients about how they should address the judge and answer any questions posed to them confidently as dictated by them. Soon the noise of the crowd had increased to a commotion, the decibel level increasing to that of a fish market till suddenly a hush fell over. The veterans sighed, the newcomers continued to chat and the chaperones shooed them to silence.

The judge followed by his attendant dressed in white and a small band of lawyers, entered the courtroom at 09.59 A.M. The attendant signaled for silence frantically before entering the courtroom and murmurs in the crowd turned to whispers. Everyone in the courtroom stood up as a sign of respect for the honorable judge. The attendant again proclaimed loudly to maintain silence and announced the commencement of the session.

The crowd gathered close to the doors of the courtroom and waited for their names to be called out by the attendant. Most of the cases were postponed to a later date for several reasons. It was as if the court existed just to announce the postponement dates and not to solve the cases. It was no wonder that there were many cases pending and people sought to settle their cases out of court in frustration. The crowd gradually thinned out. The lucky ones were the people called first while the not so fortunate had to wait the entire day.

Seetha parked her scooter inside the court compound and rushed inside at around 10.30 A.M. She knew that it was extremely late and prayed that her name should not have been called out. As soon as she reached the courtroom, she saw the crowd assembled before and snaking her way towards the entrance, her eyes searched for her lawyer and found him sitting inside the courtroom. He saw her and pointed at his watch telling her that she was late and signaled her to wait.

Someone tugged her dress and she found that it was her court companion, Meena a middle-aged woman who she had developed a friendship in the past year and sighed with relief when she learnt that her name was not called yet.

The court session continued.

She searched for a vacant seat, fully aware that she would not find any. Her legs ached after riding her scooter in the busy traffic of the city. Her daughter was sick the previous day and soon her condition worsened into a raging fever in the night. Her daughter kept her awake most of the night and Seetha finally slept at dawn when the sunlight started to seep into the house. After an hour, she was woken by her mother, who reminded that she had to be present in court in two hours. After hurrying through her morning routine, she had to skip her morning meal so that she could reach the court in time.

Her throat was parched and she thanked the Gods when she found the chaiwallah in his usual rounds selling tea in plastic cups and oily samosas. She was refreshed after drinking a cup of hot tea even though it was bad and engaged in casual conversation with Meena.

A few hours later, the judge adjourned the court for the lunch.

Seetha gathered her handbag and looked at Meena who had already started to unpack her lunch. She left after promising that she will be back on time for the afternoon session.

The board before the small hut said Janakiraman Mess which was run by an old couple. There were only a few benches and most of them were vacant. The old lady would be in her sixties but was still active, ordering her husband around the mess. Her face lit as soon as she saw Seetha parking her scooter.

Seetha smiled at the old couple after enquiring their wellbeing, she ordered her usual food: Tomato rice and pickle. There were a lot of eateries near the court but Seetha ate at Janakiraman mess even though it was far and the food was average at best. As the food was served by the old man, she remembered the first time she was here.

The district court is a place, people pass by on their way but never give a second glance and most of the people may never see the inside of the court in their lives. It is one of the most popular landmarks in the city and people when trying to give directions take it as a focal point and explain to others.

Seetha remembered her first day at court. She had not even dreamt that she would visit the court in her lifetime because hers was an orthodox middle-class family, and was taught meticulously to stay out of trouble. She had the worst case of jitters on the first day of court and clung to her parents the entire day. Her husband was waiting before the court room and on seeing her pale face, he looked at her with a devilish smile. Seetha knew that she had to face him finally. After many sleepless nights, she finally gathered her courage to attend the court session on that day, but on seeing him she felt her legs shaking. With her parent's assistance and some help from strangers, she was able to get back to her feet.

Soon she began to visit the court by herself but one fine day, she was extremely late and more nervous than usual. While driving to the court, she was feeling giddy and lost control of the vehicle. She was thrown off the scooter when it hit a lamp post and lost her consciousness as she hit the ground. Fortunately for her, an old couple was watching her the whole time, right from the time her vehicle wobbled till she fell. They immediately called for help, and with the help of the passersby, the old couple brought her to their mess and treated her with care.

Remembering the incident made her cry and controlling herself she wiped away her tears, ate quickly. After finishing her lunch, she adamantly pushed the money into the hands of the old man, who refused to accept it. For the old couple, she was like their child, a grand daughter who they never had. Seetha hurried back to the court to endure another long session till evening, but she was lucky as her name was called first. Many looked at her with envy as she left. Her case was again postponed to a later date next month.

She waited till her lawyer came looking for her.

Madame, do not lose hope. Good news is that your husband had proposed a truce through his lawyer with some conditions. So, I would suggest to consider them without making any hasty decisions.

Seetha shook her head.

Sir, the last you came carrying his white flag, his terms were preposterous and the alimony was enough to buy peanuts. Why should I even consider it now?

The lawyer persisted with a big smile.

Now, madam, your husband is more lenient in his new conditions and it would be beneficial to your family. I strongly advice that you both settle everything between yourselves since our judicial system will take its own sweet time to solve your case.

When she nodded and was about to leave, the lawyer called her and scratched his head.

How much? She asked the lawyer.

Ten thousand and do not you worry about today. We will make your husband wait for the next session.

Sir, she called him. I just want this to end as soon as possible. I have a job and a seven-year-old kid waiting for me at home. I cannot keep doing this all my life. Please. I will send the money to your wife's account as usual she replied and left.

She had been coming to the court for the last five years and was familiar with its schedule. Earlier it was a terrifying ordeal for her but now it was like visiting the local grocery.

She looked at her watch and decided that she would pick her daughter from school. After dropping her daughter at home, she decided that she could still make it to her karate class if she hurried.

Changing into her karate uniform, she started her usual routine. First was the warm up session to loosen her taut body, next she joined with the class and practiced her kathas. After her class, she started to practice with the punching bag. As she kept on kicking, she recollected the events in the past.

Eight years ago, she was waiting in a luxury hotel dressed in a traditional sari with her parents for the arrival of her future husband, Akhil. Her father had arranged the meeting as all Indian parents did. Seetha's father and Akhil's mother were colleagues working in the same bank. Akhil arrived with his parents after a few minutes. He was looking more handsome than in the picture shown by her dad.

He was talking very politely and smiled a lot at her. After some time, Seetha and Akhil were asked if they wanted to discuss anything privately.

She could not forget the rooftop restaurant where they talked for a long time about their expectations of their partner, their ambition, their hobbies, likes, and dislikes. It had started raining and they quickly moved to the shelter. She stood close to him, mesmerized by his warm nature.

She liked his personality and believed every word that he said. He spoke about equal rights for women, individuality, and freedom of speech. Moreover, he was working in a high-paying job in a software company waiting for his ticket to the US.

Seetha's parents looked at her with anxiety and were relieved when she nodded her head accepting the proposal and would regret it for a long time.

In a traditional Indian arranged marriage, the parents expect their children to decide on their life partner within a fleeting time. It is the same time it takes for pizza delivery.

Hey! Seetha. A voice brought her to reality. It was her sensei instructing her to practice a different kick.

She again started to kick the punching bag.

She was happy only for the first few months and as time passed, he started to reveal his true nature. He was a chauvinist and rarely missed the opportunity to make her feel inferior. She thought of leaving him but decided against it due to pressure from her parents & relatives. He started beating her whenever he was angry and the beatings only got worse when he was drunk.

Her malady only worsened when he lost his job, and blamed his failure on his wife. One day he hit her harder than usual and did not care as she lay in a pool of blood gasping for life. She regained her consciousness in the hospital and decided to end her marriage. Her body recovered in a month but she could not forget the pain caused by her husband.

She kicked harder and harder at the punching bag.

Seetha! Someone shouted at her.

Why don't you give it a rest? Do you want to injure your legs?

She ignored him and kept on kicking.

She filed a complaint against her husband in the local police station for harassment and applied for divorce. She had to restart her life to support herself and her son. She sought a new beginning in her life. Her childhood friend Vaani helped her to regain her foothold in society.

Five years passed swiftly. With her arduous work, she was now in a senior position in a tech firm. She was financially independent and dedicated some of her time to social work. She was also not fragile as before. Her regular visits to the gym tightened her muscles, and the karate classes she attended renewed her confidence.

She also faced a lot of difficulties in those five years. She knew how the orthodox Indian society treats an independent woman. She fought every single day in the past five years facing insults from her relatives, threats from her husband, and slanders from her work life.

Someone shook her shoulders jolting her. It was her sensei

It is time to go.

Her friend Vaani was watching her from a distance.

You practice the same thing every day. Don't you get tired?

Vaani pulled her leg.

Seetha reached her home after spending some time with Vaani. Her daughter Yaazhini ran to her and related the incidents that happened in the day at school, about her friends and their pet dog, Janu for the next hour. Seetha listened to her patiently even when her body was screaming to take rest. Finally, after putting her daughter to sleep, she climbed to the terrace and walked towards the punching bag hanging from the roof. She started her kicking routine.

After she filed the divorce case, mentioning the cruelty she had suffered by her husband's hands, her husband in turn filed a plea accusing her of mental instability, illicit relationship, and cruelty towards the in-laws. He accused her that she was not an ideal wife and a daughter-in-law.

You bastard. You asshole.

Her mind screamed with anger.

She kicked harder and harder and harder.

She waited for the day, when her husband would be punished for his sins and taken to the gallows for execution. But that day never came and she was not sure that it would come.

When she went to sleep that night, she had already decided on her next course of action.

The negotiation was arranged by the lawyers and she agreed to the measly sum of money as alimony. She stood before the judge with her head held high and accepted the annulment. As she left the court, she could feel the first day jitters returning.

Vaani was waiting for in the parking area and beckoned her to follow her quickly. They walked to the other side of the court where Seetha saw her lawyer receiving money from her ex-husband.

Swindling bastard, she cried.

Her friend, Vaani tapped her shoulder and whispered in her ear. Now is your moment.

Her ex-husband saw her and decided to throw one final insult at her before leaving.

He shouted some obscenity when he passed her and cackled.

Excuse me sir she called him.

He turned and faced her with a sarcastic smile.

Closing her eyes she inhaled deeply, bent her legs, planted her left leg firmly on the ground and slightly raised her right leg.

His eyes turned from bewilderment to shock when he saw her leg move in a flash and connect with the lower part of his body.

He collapsed on the floor clutching his balls and writhed on the floor with agony.

She left with her friend giggling like a school girl as the first raindrops fell on them.

I am hungry said Seetha. Let us have something nice to eat. Biryani?

As they were waiting for their orders in the restaurant, Seetha was watching the rain fall.

Now I know the reason why you were practicing the same kick repeatedly.

Vaani's words brought her back to reality.

You were perfecting the kick. Now I believe that even your sensei cannot match your expertise at least in this particular kick.

I literally could hear the cracking sound of his nuts.

The two friends chuckled loudly and everyone in the restaurant wondered about their sanity.

Good news reached Seetha the next day. Her kick was so strong that he had lost his manhood. An FIR was registered against her.

What are you going to do now? Her parents asked her with worry written all over their faces.

She comforted them and went to the terrace.

It was raining heavily.

Standing in the rain, she asked herself

What I am going to do?

She looked at the punching bag.

The same thing I have been doing the past couple of years.

FIGHT

RAINDROP 4

It's good to have plans and dreams, but don't be surprised if God brings you somewhere else.

Anne F. Beiler

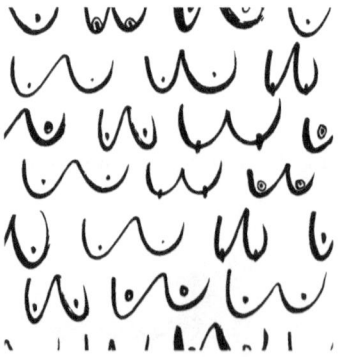

The perverted doctor

Subramani knocked on the bathroom door.

Hearing no answer from the occupant, he knocked again with frenzy.

Thud! Thud! Thud!

Open the door he shouted and kept knocking.

The old wooden door creaked loudly and the hinges seemed to come loose.

Stop it you moron cried his sister Dhanalakshmi from inside the bathroom. Can't you wait for five minutes?

It's already late. The show starts at 10 and it is already eight-thirty. You very well know that there are no direct buses to the movie theater will take around an hour by bus if there are no traffic jams, processions, and another ten-minute walk.

You could have started early, his sister retorted.

I had to run some errands for Kittu Mama. He wanted some letters to be posted urgently, today of all days and he could not find someone else to do it. Will you stop talking and get out.

It is your mouth which is blabbering since morning. You do not have the right to order me, just because you are going to become a doctor. I am still your elder sister.

Subramani hailed from a middle-class family and was the fourth child. He was the only son of the Sundaresan family. The elder daughters Meenakshi and Vanathi were already married. They were software professionals and had shifted to the US with their husbands. His sister Dhanalakshmi was one year older and was pursuing second-year computer engineering in a popular engineering college in Chennai. Since Subramani was the only boy, he was pampered by his parents.

His father, Sundaresan, was an engineer working in the PWD department in Chepauk, Chennai city and his wife Kamatchi was a homemaker. He was earning a good salary but he had spent most of his savings for his two daughters' marriages. Also, he was about to retire in two years.

Subramani was highly intelligent and had been the first in his class since fifth grade in his school. When he cleared the medical entrance in flying colors and was allocated a seat in the prestigious Madras Medical College, his parents were overjoyed. He would be the only doctor in his family.

Why the hurry? You will miss the show anyhow. Dhanalakshmi teased him when she left the bathroom.

Subramani hit her head and entered the bathroom.

He heard his sister complain to his mother and her mother calming her as he poured the water on his head. His sister's complaints continued now to his father as he ate his breakfast. When he left the house, his sister was shouting that they were always supporting him even when he was at fault. He smiled and hurried to the bus stop near his house. By the time he reached the theatre, the show had already started. His college mate Manikandan his childhood friend since kindergarten was waiting for him and he looked as if he had swallowed a pineapple.

Do you know how hard it was for me to get the tickets to this movie?

'Pannadai' was the title of the movie, which was a huge hit and had become immensely popular with the youth. It was the lead actor's third movie; the first movie was Mollamaari and the second was Mudhichavukki. Huge posters screamed the actor's name as the Young Mega Maga Everlasting Phenomenal Star Sonamuthu and predicted that he was the next super star and the future chief minister. The young heroes of Indian film industry seemed to run out of titles before their names.

Manikandan and Subramanian rushed inside avoiding collision with the crowd coming out after watching the movie, some of them slapping themselves for wasting time and money on such a terrible movie. I am sure by now we would have missed the important introduction fight scene in the film where the hero breaks open the iron door and thrashes the Goondas for harassing his sister. Manikandan was a diehard fan of the lead actor in the film and he did not want to miss even a single scene of his Thalaivar's movie.

Subramanian entered the dimly lit theatre and switched on the light in his mobile phone to find the seats allocated to them. He had to drag his friend as he searched for their seats since his friend was already engrossed in the movie, watching his favorite hero thrash the rowdies. Finding their seats, he was about to switch off the light when he saw the front row was occupied by college girls wearing modern clothes. He saw the girl in front of his seat was wearing a low-neck top and he could see some cleavage. His blood boiled as he strained his eyes when he heard people shouting at him to sit. He sighed and sat down knowing that he would not watch the movie that day but try to get a good look at the girl's cleavage. He was disappointed that it was not visible in the dark.

The heroine's introduction scene distracted him for a while as the hero was watching the heroine bathing in the waterfalls. The director of the movie made sure to show many close-up shots of the heroine's cleavage and the hero's face ogling at the heroine. There was a huge applause from the audience when the hero compared the heroine's assets to fruits. Next came the song describing the heroine and the hero's intention of preparing a Cocktail using the heroine's fruits. The others were thoroughly enjoying the movie except Subramani who yearned for even a tiny glance at the girl's cleavage in front of his seat.

He remembered the time when he went with his schoolmates to an adult movie in a dinghy theatre that smelled like cum. It was the first time he saw the breasts of a woman and his days of perversion started from that day.

The movie screen showed Interval in block letters and the lights in the cinema hall turned on.

Let us get some snacks urged Manikandan. The samosas here are world famous, and I am so hungry after such a marvelous first half that I am sure that the second half will be explosive. I am anxiously waiting for the helicopter chase scene, the underwater fight scene, the bull fighting scene and the hot scenes between the hero and the heroine.

Subramani shook his head. Can you get some strong tea for me because I have developed a strong headache after watching the first half and If I want to survive the movie post interval, I need aspirin which I fortunately carry with me everywhere.

Stop cussing, asshole. You will not get anything to eat if you do not accompany me shouted Manikandan.

Alright, I will come. Subramani slowly raised himself looking at the girl in front of him out of the corner of his eye. As long as you do not start glorifying your hero, he continued. I came because I like the heroine and I heard that her performance in this movie was exemplary.

Subramani was about to follow Manikandan when the girl stood and turned towards him. She then bent to search for something on her seat. He would have shouted eureka as her cleavage now widened till, he could see a lot more things. Did Time seemed to stand still or was it Subramani who stood motionless staring anxiously.

The girl realized suddenly that she had been careless and pulled her tops at the same time checking her surroundings. She saw Subramani watching her with no shame.

Bastard, she cried and sat down. Her friends turned back to look at him angrily and were arguing amongst themselves. The person in the back seat tapped his shoulder. Did you have a wonderful time, brother? He asked with a laugh.

The movie ended as usual, the hero killing everyone except the Villain, whose life is spared because he turns over a new leaf after orchestrating the murder of many and because he turns out to be his brother. The heroine's role was only to romanticize with the hero and to show her assets in the songs. Subramani hastened his friend to leave who did not budge from his seat.

As Subramani was about to leave, the girl confronted him.

Did you get a good look at my boobs? Or should I bend once more if you did not. Is it as good as your sister? You fucking pervert.

Subramani bit his tongue and dragged his friend away from her.

What did you do? Manikandan asked him.

It was pouring when Subramani reached home.

He saw his sister waiting for him on the porch and realized that she was crying.

Dhanalakshmi wiped away her tears when he opened the gate and rushed towards him.

Do you know how ashamed I was when my friend called and said about the disgusting incident in the theatre? How could you behave like that? She asked him angrily.

He averted her eyes and stared at the ground. He tried to deny it at first but soon gave up after his sister narrated the entire incident.

Did you tell father? Subramani asked her with fear.

How could I tell them? She looked at him with repugnance. Now my friends would never visit me and I will be the laughing stock of the college if everyone knows that I have a pervert brother. She left him standing in the rain.

He knew that he had a big problem as he tried to sleep and made up his mind to restrain himself from the next day. The dreams he had that night proved him wrong. The girl who had sat in front of his seat was more than willing to show her breasts. He twisted and turned as she appeared in different outfits begging him to measure her bust size.

His mobile rang at 6 A.M. the next day. It was his elder sisters on a conference call. After listening to their lecture for an hour and apologizing to them profusely, he was let off with a warning. He knew in his heart that he would never change his ways and had to be more careful in the future.

Time passed swiftly.

Subramani was in his second year of college. In the first year, he tried his best to be discreet when watching the girls in his college. He understood that his father was struggling to run the family, pay the tuition fee of his two children and manage the household expenses as well. The only way he could repay his father was to perform well in the exams. He put aside his childish fantasies and devoted most of his time preparing for the final exams. When the first-year results were announced, his name was on the top of the list. His parents were overjoyed and his sister spoke to him jovially as old times.

He managed to befriend many classmates who often visited him for clarifying their doubts and the professors were pleased with his dedication. Without any doubt, he was the most popular in his class. But soon things took a bad turn when he fell in bad company.

He was so obsessed with boobs that he could easily guess the exact size just by looking. Finding his talent, his friends decided to test him. The game started casually in the beginning when he was asked to guess the breast size of the girls walking past them. But soon the other boys asked him to guess their girlfriend's size to gift them lingerie as a surprise. When his predictions came true, he was given more challenges like guessing the sizes of the professors which included some males, the fat ones who resembled Eddie Murphy in the movie 'Nutty professor'

His fame spread everywhere and most of the students knew about his weird talent. As he became more obsessed with accepting more ordeals, he did not realize many of the girls shunned away from him and the professors, who had cared for him once, now treated him with cold indifference.

His popularity became his bane.

Whenever any harassment was reported by the girls, he was suspected to be the culprit. Although he just liked to watch the boobs and never crossed the line, his name popped up in everyone's mind.as the prime suspect.

The engineering college where his sister studied were conducting their annual cultural event and invitations were sent to many colleges including Madras Medical College to participate. Subramani went to the event with his friends Manikandan, Suresh, and their girlfriends Gomathi and Lavanya. The event was a tremendous success as a multitude of students visited the event and everyone enjoyed the different shows performed on the stage. Subramani was busy judging the breast sizes of the girls and was astonished to find that his fame had to spread to other colleges too. Alas he had an appointment the next morning so he had to cut short his visit and returned home.

He entered the college premises the next day and noticed many students talking in hushed tones and, glared at him as he passed. Even the professors looked at him with suspicion. Only after reaching his class, he realized that his name was being suspected by many students. During the event, some of the students heard a girl scream from one of the deserted classrooms and decided to investigate. The girl was found half-dazed in a dark place, her clothes in rags, exposing skin in many places and howling in pain. An unknown person had forced her and attempted to rape her. She could not recollect his face since it was dark.

She lodged a formal complaint in the police station the next day. Unfortunately, the thing which she remembered the last before the incident was Subramani ogling at her boobs trying to guess her size at the request of his friends.

The entire college stood before their classes when the police came. The crowd gasped when Subramani was asked to report immediately to the Dean's office.

Subramanian walked to the Dean's office with fear and looked at the faces of his fellow students watching him like an insect. He thought he was being punished without even a trial. After a brief inquiry, he was let off the hook because he had a solid alibi during the incident.

Subramani's woes did not end that day as many students still believed that he was the culprit. An internal inquiry was conducted by the college where his previous misdeeds were scrutinized by the faculty before his parents and concluded that he might have been capable to do such a devious thing. Sundaresan and his wife were devastated and they uttered not a single word during the entire inquiry. They did not even flinch when their son was suspended till, he was proven not guilty.

His father exploded in tears as soon as they reached home and suddenly his mother fainted. Subramani could not believe the series of events that was happening that was not his fault but he never lost hope. With grit determination, he took control of the situation and his bereaving family.

Subramani was again summoned by the inquiry board and after a stern warning, he was asked to attend the classes from the next day. The culprit was still not found. Subramani attended the classes the next day and saw his friends withdrew from him. Even his close friend Manikandan shunned away, abandoning him in his solitude. He knew that he was being called a dirty pervert behind his back and noticed that girls adjusting their dress when he crossed them.

The bell chimed in the evening signaling the end of the day and Subramani left his classroom alone. As he crossed the playground, a couple of boys confronted him with hockey sticks and started hitting him black and blue. One of them was the assaulted girl's brother and he had come with his friends to teach him a lesson. Neither his fellow students nor his friends interfered. He fell on the ground with blood streaming from his face and watched his assaulters leave.

The first few drops fell on him and it started raining. The rainwater cooled his burning body and quenched his thirst. He watched the rain falling from a great height and the black clouds moving at great speed across the sky as he lay on the wet ground. He saw a crowd of faces gather around him and blocking his view of the sky. The view blurred as he slipped into unconsciousness.

Twenty years later

California, Los Angeles.

Manikandan was driving his Audi Q7 in the busy streets of the city teeming with tourists from every corner of the world. He was a successful surgeon and had settled in the US with his wife who was a pediatrician. Traffic was heavier than ever and he realized that his plans to reach home a little early go down the drain. Because of his busy schedule Manikandan rarely could spend time with his family so he tried to find every opportunity to be with them. He was very tired as he waited for the traffic to clear and tried hard to drive under the legal speed. His body had already gone into backup mode after working long hours in the hospital. His prognosis was that if he continued this existence his heart would soon give away.

As the traffic moved, he heard the distinct noise of a sports car throttling next to him. He turned and saw a beautiful red Ferrari convertible being driven by an Indian man wearing expensive clothes.

Lucky bastard, he declared. Must be a geek from Silicon Valley.

As he moved the car, he saw the driver of the Ferrari waving at him and could not believe his eyes when he found that the man was his old friend, Subramani. He followed the car to a fancy pub and Subramani invited him for a few beers.

Manikandan knew that Subramani was ridiculed by everyone after the incident at the cultural event. His grades were poor and barely managed to complete the medical course. His family shifted to another city and no one knew what he had become. No one bothered to find where Subramani went including Manikandan.

Manikandan thought about his friend for a few years but time erased his existence from his mind. He was shocked to see him in an expensive car after he had assumed that he would be working for scraps somewhere in a remote village in India.

Subramani ordered an expensive scotch for both. Manikandan shook his head and ordered a beer. Subramani enquired his friend whether he was avoiding hard liquor. Manikandan shook his head. Subramani insisted that it was his treat and ordered the whiskey. The two friends talked of old times and Manikandan avoided speaking about the incident. After a lengthy conversation, the friends parted on their ways.

Manikandan saw the card given to him by Subramani. His residential address showed that it was in Beverly Hills where most of the celebrities call their homes. He sent a message to his wife about the reunion with his friend.

The next day was the week off so Manikandan was sleeping late in the morning when his wife shook him awake. His friends from his college days had assembled in his house and everyone was waiting for him. When he entered the living room, they surrounded him and started enquiring about his friend. Manikandan showed him the card which just mentioned his friend's name, his mobile number, and his home address.

They bombarded him with questions.

Where does he work?

What is he doing in the US?

When did he come?

Where did he steal the car?

Did he marry a rich girl and settle here? And the final question was.

Who will marry the dirty pervert?

Manikandan did not know the answers so to clarify their doubts, they asked Manikandan to invite him for a reunion at a popular pub called Big Knockers near Beverly hills.

Manikandan beamed with pride when Subramani accepted his offer and agreed to meet him at the golf course nearby.

Manikandan reached the golf club with his friends frequented by the rich and the glamorous. The security stopped their car and let them on their way once they mentioned Subramani's name. Subramani was waiting for them in the posh restaurant within the golf club. Manikandan and his friends hugged him like old comrades. They had forgotten that he was a dirty pervert. Finally, someone mentioned the incident that happened during their college days and a string of questions continued.

Where did you go after college?

What did you specialize in?

When did you move to the US?

Where are you working now? Which hospital?

Are you married or a bachelor? And the final question was.

Did you realize your mistakes and stop being a pervert?

Subramani's phone beeped.

I am sorry guys, he said. One of my wealthy clients has shown up at my clinic and demanding my presence. My clinic is on the way to the pub and I will join you as soon as I can. Manikandan's friends saw the black Lamborghini carrying Subramani kick dust and sped off.

One of the gangs pointed that the clinic was in one of the costliest real estates of the city.

Why do not we surprise him at his clinic, Manikandan suggested which was readily accepted by everyone. Hey followed him to his clinic which occupied the entire floor in one of the high-rise buildings in the city. A receptionist who looked like the perfect likeness to Angelina Jolie smiled at them when they approached the desk.

Please wait in the adjacent room. Dr. Subramani is busy with another patient and will be with you in a short while. The duplicate Angelina Jolie listened to their request and answered in a husky voice.

After waiting for an hour, Subramani apologized for the tardiness and personally invited them to his office decorated with enlarged photos of women's breasts.

Subramani smiled when they looked at each other and continued.

The answer to your question of whether I have stopped being a pervert is a big NO. But I am making money from it now, a shitload of money because all my clients are rich celebrities. I alter their shapes and make them beautiful, he pointed at the pictures of the breasts. I am enjoying my work and my life without any commitments. My wife is a supermodel who is right now shooting for a commercial in Buenos Aires. My parents are living very comfortably in the four-bedroom mansion, I had bought for them a few miles from here and my sister is working in NASA.

His friends realized that Subramani had a far better life than them. As Manikandan was leaving, Subramani asked him whether he wanted the tickets for the super bowl the next day as he had another appointment. Manikandan saw that they were premium tickets and accepted them without shame.

As Manikandan left with his friends, it had started raining. He saw that Subramani was standing on the balcony of his office, enjoying the rain.

RAINDROP 5

All men dream, but not equally.
Those who dream by night in the dusty recesses of their minds, wake in the day to find that it was vanity; but the dreamers of the day are dangerous men, for they may act on their dreams with open eyes, to make them possible.

T. E. Lawrence

Heads or tails

Somewhere in Romania

Ivanovich a 60-year-old well-built Ukranian climbed the 150-step circular stairway to the top of the keep and calmly observed the bustling activity happening in the dead of the night. The keep was the tallest tower in the Vlad castle which provided a bird's eye view of its surroundings. The castle was constructed on top of a mountain, protected by sheer drops and accessible only by the twisting road from the sleepy village at the foot of the mountain whose inhabitants were poor farmers depending on the castle for their livelihoods. In exchange the villagers served as watchdogs who communicated the happenings in the vicinity to the castle.

Even in the middle of the night, he could see the four outer watchtowers and the men walking the length of the walkways connecting the towers, the big courtyard, the postern gate, and the drawbridge connecting the castle with the road from the village. He smiled when he saw the line of moving lights crawling up the mountain like a snake and readied himself to welcome his guests. He climbed down the spiral stairs, reached the base of the tower, and checked with his head of security to ensure everything was progressing smoothly. The castle could defend itself against an army and a garrison of highly professional mercenaries always kept vigil. At any time 20 men manned the watchtowers, 10 men stood watch in the courtyard and 10 men patrolled the perimeter with additional 10 men stationed in the Barbican, a fortified gatehouse at the entrance of the castle.

Ivanovich entered the main hall which was once the throne room of a boyar now converted into an opulent Victorian ball room. He had spared no expense to decorate it. Patterned wallpapers, rich vibrant tapestries, fleur-de-lis medallions, garlands and wreaths decorated the walls and the ceiling was covered by colorful frescoes depicting the great hunt.

The guests had already parked their expensive cars in the courtyard and underwent the security formalities. Then they were guided by handsome waiters to the ballroom and taken to their allotted seats. The ballroom was now being readied for a different purpose. A makeshift elevated stage was erected in the center of the room that can be viewed clearly from everywhere in the room and round tables were arranged meticulously around the stage. The ballroom was dimly lit except for the focus light that illuminated the stage as bright as day.

When every guest had been comfortably seated with their preferred drinks, Ivanovich rang the bell and listed down the rules to be followed, the penalties for non-compliance among other things. He looked at the people from different races of the world; the only similarity was they were filthy rich and the scum of humanity. A Babel of voices was heard spoken by different tongues and a hush fell when the bell was rung twice indicating the start of the bidding.

A group of girls, who had just entered puberty, barely covered in transparent veils waited near the stage to display their bodies to the anxious spectators. As each girl stood on the stage, twisted, and turned, a base price was announced for the purchase of the girl followed by the boisterous bids from the crowd. The girl became the property of the highest bidder.

After two hours the bidding finally ended after most of the girls were sold like cattle. The guests departed with their prized possessions and left in their fancy rides. The few unfortunate girls who failed to impress the guests were offered to the mercenaries and they would not survive the night. By the look on Ivanovich's face, anyone could guess that everything had proceeded brilliantly. He took out his mobile phone, punched some numbers and waited for the answer from the other side.

Sir, how are you? Everything went well over there.

The voice from the other side spoke with a heavy Indian accent.

Quit talking and tell me when I can expect my shipment?

Ivanovich barked angrily.

It is being readied as we speak and will reach your place in a month, Sir. Don't you worry; everything will go according to plan. The voice now stuttered back with fear.

See that you do. Ivanovich replied and cut the call.

Penthouse, Luxe Towers,

Malabar hill, Mumbai

An elephant of a man heard the call disconnect on the other side and threw the phone angrily.

How dare he cut me like that? What does he think of me? He may be a big man in his country but I am the Badshah of Mumbai. Tara Singh, one of the most powerful figures in the Mumbai underworld bellowed

Anwar, what happened to the goods?

The giant looked at his subordinate and demanded.

The thin subordinate stood respectfully and replied that the goods were on its way from the four corners of India and will reach the warehouse on the first week of July.

Call all our agents shouted Tara Singh and ask them to move their asses. The next auction date has already been confirmed and we must make sure the shipment reaches its destination on time. And make sure the goods are undamaged and satisfy the age criteria. They must be virgins who had just started to bleed, with pretty faces. If our goods do not meet their criteria, our client will cancel our partnership in the blink of an eye. So, make sure our agents understand it clearly.

Anwar nodded his head and proceeded to the balcony that offered breathtaking views of the Arabian sea. Signaling the servant to bring him some Tea and snacks, he settled himself comfortably in the swing sofa and started making calls.

Chembur, Mumbai

The high-pitched siren noise from the next room interrupted Salim and drove him mad but he couldn't ignore it since it was the ring tone he had set for the most important callers. The nude girl on the bed urged him to continue but he had already risen and with significant effort pried himself free from the girl's grasp. He found the phone and recognizing the number on the screen, answered it immediately. He went to the balcony of his flat occupying the fifteenth floor of the building and looked at the surroundings. The scenery here was in stark contrast with the one seen by Anwar

Salaam, Anwar Bhai. What is your command? He listened to the response.

Yes Bhai, I understand clearly? He replied. Pretty Virgins and Undamaged.

Got it he said. 100% Pukka Bhai.

He cut the call and looked down at the slum below dotted by shacks. He climbed down the stairs of the building and walked down the narrow street littered with garbage and entered one of the shacks.

A group of thugs were watching a soccer match and on seeing him stood up with respect.

The delivery date has been preponed. We must make sure the goods are packed and ready for dispatch.

Anwar also made calls to other places all over India and confirmed their commitments.

One week before the delivery date, a call from Delhi was received by the commissioner of police, Coimbatore city. When the commissioner answered the call, the voice on the other end introduced itself as Sigma from the CID office in Delhi. It proceeded to tell that there have been rumors about a smuggling ring planning to kidnap many young girls from different corners of India and ship them to some foreign buyer. Also, investigations were underway to find the mastermind of the operation and the members, their routes, and the mode of delivery. The voice also instructed the commissioner to assemble a team to investigate the recent missing person cases in the city.

A few minutes after the call from the CID office ended, Inspector Hari hurried to the secluded spot behind the commissioner's office and made a call. A feminine voice on the other end said Minister's office, May I know who is on the line and the purpose of your call. Inspector Hari introduced himself and ordered the girl to connect him immediately to the minister. When the call was put through, a jarring voice spoke from the other end.

I am a little busy right now discussing some serious issues with the leader of our party's women's wing so call after an hour will you. Hari knew about the minister and the kind of discussions he had with the members of the women's wing. Sorry to disturb your schedule but the CID dogs have caught the scent of the kidnappings and they also alerted the Commissioner's office.

After a long time, the minister answered

I will contact Salim and relay your message. Make sure to alert our agents to proceed with utmost caution.

Salim nodded as he spoke to the minister.

I understand. It is not new for us, right. You do your part and we will do ours. On the day of the transport, inform our contact and make sure the check posts are manned by the people on our payroll.

Fucking Madrasi. Salim spat on the ground when the call ended.

The day of the shipment neared.

The secret warehouse near Nagpur in the middle of a slum inhabited by robbers and cutthroats waited silently to receive its goods. At that time, the whole neighborhood would be on its toes, watching for police and making sure none of the girls escape. Most of the young girls who were being kidnapped were from poor families whose complaints were either simply ignored or registered as eloping or run-away cases. Huge networks of people all over India were working without rest at the command of Tara Singh to deliver the goods.

Townhall, Coimbatore

David walked with a brisk pace on the platform occupied by peddlers, slipping between the mad rush of other commuters from the opposite direction. It was busy as usual and the people crisscrossed the streets casually ignoring the motorists honking their horns loudly. As he passed the P1 police station, he heard the cries of a woman and saw a crowd watching the commotion happening inside. Curiosity tugged him and made him stand with the crowd. He waited till the cries became louder and watched an old couple come out of the station with tears streaming from their eyes. The crowd continued to watch as the couple stood outside the police station David watched them looking back at the police station as if expecting some miracle and finding none they continued to wait. David walked towards them.

What happened? He asked the couple wearing rags.

They shook their heads and continued their way. Suddenly the wife lost her balance and fell to the ground unconscious. A crowd soon gathered around them. The fifty-year-old police officer on guard outside the station rushed inside and related the incident to his superior who promptly responded to ignore.

David immediately went to the petty shop nearby and returned with a bottle of soda. He sprinkled some on the lady's face. She slowly regained consciousness and accepted the soda from David. The crowd dispersed when it thought there will not be any excitement after that.

The husband took David's hands and placed them on his eyes when the first of the raindrops fell.

Thank you very much, son said the old man, with a shaky voice. It started to rain heavily as if the sky itself felt pity for the couple.

David took the couple to a tea shop and ordered tea and snacks for them.

I am David, a member of the Joint hands club doing social work in Coimbatore. We do everything from planting trees to giving free legal advice to the downtrodden members of this society. If you have any problem, you can tell me.

The husband looked into his eyes and finding nothing but compassion, he opened his mouth to talk.

My 12-year-old daughter who was working in a factory nearby did not return for two days. We enquired everywhere but did not get any positive response. The police did not even register an FIR at first and presumed that she eloped with someone. But after convincing them for two days, they finally registered the complaint but I doubt that they will seriously investigate the case.

His wife shook her head and waved angrily at her husband.

He forced our daughter to quit school and work at the textile mill even though she was a bright student. Her ambition was to become a doctor and serve the downtrodden members of the society. I could not make enough money to satisfy my husband who always needed more to drink and gamble. She sacrificed her dreams to protect me from his wrath and started stitching clothes instead of people's wounds. I almost collapsed when the police suggested that she would have eloped with someone but I know my daughter would never do that, not in a million years. She goes from home to the factory and comes back right after her shift like clockwork My gut says that someone had kidnapped her and I do not know whether she is alive or not. How will I convince the police that she did not run away and persuade them to search for her.

David consoled them that he would do everything in his power to find the girl. He then took them to his office and introduced them to the president of the club. Sahayam, a man in his sixties who was the president of the Joint hands' social welfare club received the couple with open hands and assured them that come hell or high water he would do everything in his power to help them.

The Joint hands club joined with other welfare clubs organized a protest in front of the commissioner's office demanding justice for the poor couple and highlighted that many girls from poor backgrounds had disappeared in the city. The police so far had not done their duties and are continually ignoring the pleas of the poor. Noone took the protests seriously including the police who continued to do their duties as usual. The people passing on the road did not even bother to listen to the commotion thinking that it was not their concern. All it took was a matchstick and a can of fuel to pull everyone's attention towards the protests.

An old man ran to the front of the crowd with a kerosene can and set himself on fire before anyone could respond. The crowd dispersed as the burning man ran amok and by the time the police officers came to their senses, it was too late. The media soon converged on the scene like wolves. News reporters clicked pictures of the body burning on the road, the crowd running in every direction, and the police officers watching the proceedings like statues. Soon the protests would be broadcasted on many news channels

As the news spread like wild fire more people joined the protests and even the people passing through the streets chanted slogans along with the protestors. Many students from various parts of the state arrived En masse and joined the protests. Heated debates raged across the whole nation, many agreeing to the gradual deterioration of law & order while others argued that it was a publicity stunt.

The protesters did not budge even when the commissioner appealed to the crowd that he will take responsibility and ensure that the children would be found and reunited with their parents. It was rumored that the protests would soon turn into riots and soon it became true when some of the mob stoned the vehicles passing by.

A fleet of cars arrived and stopped before the commissioner's office like clockwork and the familiar face of the minister of law-and-order Mr.Ammaiappan could be seen through the windows. The police men formed a human chain serving as a barrier between the minister's car and the crowd which seemed to break at any time against the onslaught of the crowd. A loudspeaker was quickly given to the minister and with his trademark voice, the minister welcomed the people.

The crowd calmed after hearing the minister's captivating speech and appealed that it was the work of superior caste people. The situation had quickly turned into a racist problem.

The minister convinced them that he would do everything in his power to bring back the girls and he was even prepared to fight singlehandedly with Yama, the God of death. He also added that if the previous government had taken steps towards security, this would not have happened. Now it became a political issue as people blamed the opposite party for its negligence.

Hari watched the protests and narrated the incidents to someone on the phone. The situation will soon be under control. The minister had cleverly diverted the people's minds. Soon the people will forget about this incident and continue with their pathetic lives.

Meanwhile container lorries from various parts of the country started on their long journey to the secret warehouse one week before delivery. One of the Lorries from Coimbatore was approaching the check post near Mettur when it was stopped by the police. The police officer on duty summoned the driver and questioned him about its destination. After receiving a bundle of currency, he was allowed to leave. The lorry then continued its journey carrying its valuable cargo and crossed many such check points unhindered with the power of money.

Investigative journalists uncovered a substantial number of kidnappings that occurred in recent times with the common characteristic being the abductees were mostly girls between the ages of 12 and 15. They also declared that most of those cases were either closed as eloping or ignored by the police which left a serious doubt about the effectiveness of the police force in people's minds.

The ramifications of the protests had not dissipated before another shocking incident threw the Tamil Nadu state police force in a state of turmoil.

Inspector Hari rushed to the minister's house when he heard about the disappearance of the minister's granddaughter. Many of the senior police officers were already there consoling the grieving parents. The twelve-year girl was dropped at the ballet dance academy by the car driver and she was last seen leaving the academy with a couple of friends. The car driver waited for a long time before the academy for her to return but when she did not, he promptly informed the girl's parents. Even after the academy and the surroundings were searched thoroughly no one knew where she went and she had vanished into thin air The entire police department was alerted and every exit out of the city was locked down. Every vehicle that exited the city was thoroughly searched and new check posts erected in important junctions within the city ensured that the kidnappers cannot transport the girl without alerting the authorities. Every traffic cam, CCTVs under the control of the government were examined by the police for any clues.

My granddaughter should be at home by evening or many heads will roll, the minister threatened the police. The next day, a ransom note was found inside the newspaper, delivered to the minister's house demanding 50 crores as payment failing which the girl would be returned in pieces.

The police scratched their heads to find the source of the ransom note and subsequently it was traced to the Joint hands social club which they raided in the dead of the night. But the girl was not found after searching every nook and corner of the building and the canine squad was useless because the dogs did not find the scent of the girl. Every member of the group was rounded up and taken to a warehouse used by the police for interrogating terrorists.

Inspector Hari thought that he had entered a madhouse when he saw the members of the Joint hands social club being subjected to inhuman torture and he approached the minister overseeing the savagery, shouting orders to inflict maximum pain to the culprits.

Sir, he spoke in his ears. Can you order the men to stop torturing them?

The minister turned towards him and spat on his face.

How dare you interfere? You son of a bitch. I will find my granddaughter even if I must skin every one of them alive. If you can't stomach it, get out of my way or else you will join them.

Listen to me you, moron, shouted Inspector Hari. You won't get the truth from them no matter what you do.

The minister was stunned for a second but in an instant, he took a revolver and pointed at the inspector's forehead.

How dare you? You, filthy dog whom I raised from the streets.

Sir, pleaded the Inspector. They are one of our money machines, the agents which I hire to kidnap the girls. I have been using them for many years and I can vouch for their loyalty.

What? Cried the minister and dropped the gun.

The inspector continued. Sir, the joint hands club is just a front for our illegal activities and their key role is to abduct the girls. We collect the girls and deliver them to Tara Singh. So, they wouldn't dare to lay their hands on your family because they know the consequences. They were setup by someone who has a fair knowledge of our dealings.

We must identify the person who actually kidnapped your granddaughter, the inspector persisted. Let us proceed with caution.

The ringing sound from the inspector's phone interrupted his conversation. Inspector Hari knew that it was his mistress and cut the call. But the phone started to ring again.

Answer the bloody phone ordered the minister.

Apologizing to the minister, Inspector Hari pressed the Answer button and pressed the receiver to his ear.

What the fuck are you doing? The voice on the other end shouted. Our daughter has not come home after school. I have already checked with the school and was calling her friends to find her whereabouts when the servant came to me with a ransom note demanding 10 crores for our daughter's life. Are the police doing their duty or not? With all the news about the kidnappings, I am very scared that she may be one of the victims.

What the hell are you talking about? The inspector roared like a maniac.

The call from the kidnapper was received by the minister and the inspector after a day demanding whether they had arranged the money. The voice was muffled to prevent identification and the call was disconnected just before it could be traced. The minister had spared no expense and had deployed a huge group of people from diverse backgrounds to find the kidnapper. Police officers, rowdies, informers, private eyes, and Techies worked day and night to find the girls.

When all the minister's efforts bore no fruit, the case was transferred to the CBI. A highly capable officer Mr. Narayanan Kutty who had solved many cases before and helped nab dangerous criminals was delegated to find the kidnappers. He was given carte blanche in his investigation and was allowed to pick the liaisons from the local police.

After scrutinizing the case files, he found many discrepancies. The kidnappers seemed in no hurry to get the money because they hadn't mentioned a deadline for delivering the money. Also, he was intrigued by the timeframe of the kidnapping and his instincts told him that he was not looking at the big picture. He understood that something was missing

So, their motive may not be money asked the minister.

Narayanan Kutty was deep in his thoughts when the question jolted him back to reality. He took a sip of the tea and found that it had gone cold.

The minister ordered a fresh cup of tea by reading his face.

What is your next step asked the minister

I am intrigued by the date of the kidnapping. Both the girls, your granddaughter, and the inspector's daughter were nabbed on the same day. If the same person had managed to kidnap both the girls, then he should have abundant resources at his disposal. It is not child's play to abduct two girls in the same day and hide them from the police for so long. He had managed to hide his tracks so far but as per the adage, 'Even an elephant's foot will slip' so I am waiting for the kidnappers to make the tiniest mistake so that I can use it to our advantage.

Narayanan Kutty paused before continuing. Because I believe that 'Even a tiny blade of grass is a powerful weapon in the hands of a valiant man.'

Another proverb, the minister asked sarcastically. So are you planning to wait for the kidnappers to make a mistake.

On the contrary replied Narayanan Kutty, I think we must act fast to find both the girls because they may be smuggled outside the country. Haven't you received the intelligence report from the crime branch regarding the shipment of girls within the next two weeks.

Narayanan Kutty continued, if an international network of criminals were indeed behind the kidnappings, then it would have been a cinch to kidnap both the girls since they have many people in India occupying high level positions in their payroll.

One week had passed and the container Lorries with the girls had reached their destination. The girls were then shifted to the warehouse and they were asked to remove all their clothes. When they cried with fear, the leader of the group assured them that no harm would come to them if they stayed inside the warehouse. He also warned them that they were in the middle of the slum of rapists so he could not guarantee their safety if they tried to get outside without their clothes.

One of his men approached.

Did you check the inventory?

The leader asked him.

The man leered and showed two fingers.

The leader laughed. The more the better. Boss will be pleased.

Tara Singh was relaxing in the rooftop spa of a luxury hotel when he saw his thin subordinate approach him nonchalantly.

Did the goods reach our place safely? Were there any complications?

Tara Singh enquired anticipating his response.

Everything is fine sir replied Anwar.

Don't be so overconfident snubbed Tara Singh. I wouldn't be so sure till the goods are safely onboard the cargo ship enroute to Romania.

Meanwhile in Coimbatore....

There was no further communication from the kidnapper. The police were at their wit's end and the minister seemed to explode at any time.

Narayanan Kutty visited the minister's office asking to speak to him personally.

The minister showed him a big briefcase filled with money.

Take this and find my granddaughter, he said. This is just an advance and you will get thrice this amount if you manage to deliver her safely.

Sir, said Narayanan Kutty. Have some confidence in the police department. It is my duty to find the girls and I will find them no matter what. My duty to bring the kidnappers to justice motivates me more than your money. So please don't belittle me and take away your money. We suspect that Tara Singh, a notorious arms dealer, who controls one of the biggest crime syndicates in India is the mastermind behind the kidnapping network but we are yet to find concrete evidence. Also, through one of our detectives, we found that they are being held in a secret place somewhere in the state of Maharashtra but we couldn't pinpoint its exact location. They may smuggle them outside the country within the next few days.

The minister broke down in tears.

It's impossible shouted the minister. The girls who were kidnapped by them were from poor backgrounds. Why should they abduct my granddaughter. Since you didn't do your job properly, you are trying to link both the cases.

Narayanan Kutty listened to the minister's charade patiently.

Sir, I am happy that you know a great deal about the smugglers' modus of operandi but I would like to point a few details that will intrigue you.

He paused to see the minister's reaction and continued.

On the date of the kidnapping, a mysterious container lorry had crossed many check posts before crossing Tamil Nadu state border by bribing the police officers in the check post. We suspect that the lorry was used to transport the girls. We have traced its route till it entered Maharashtra after crossing Karnataka but it disappeared without a trace after taking a detour in Nagpur. If we find the lorry, we would have found your granddaughter and the other girls.

Narayanan Kutty saluted and left.

Inspector Hari dressed as a businessperson cleared the security at the Dr. Babasaheb Ambedkar International Airport and was welcomed by a scorching heatwave as he exited the airport. He wiped the sweat that seemed to pour from his forehead as he waited for the contact to arrive.

A black Land rover pulled near him and the driver rolled down the dark tinted windows.

Inspector Hari calmly walked to the SUV.

Do you know the best place in this town to eat fried chicken? He enquired the driver casually.

I know just the place; the driver said without emotion and signaled him to get inside the car.

The SUV exited the airport and reached the highway. After zigzagging through the traffic for a few miles, it exited the highway and entered a mud road. It raised the dust as the driver expertly maneuvered the SUV in the narrow road riddled with potholes. The inspector saw a small settlement in the distance and deduced that they were nearing their destination and the warehouse would be somewhere nestled inside the settlement. The SUV soon reached the settlement and stopped near the temporary check post manned by ruffians. After inspecting the vehicle, the ruffians allowed the SUV to proceed inside the settlement.

The inspector found that the people who were the scum of the society lived in shacks made of metal sheets throughout the settlement. The narrow lane twisted and turned before it reached a clearing in the middle of the slum where the warehouse was located and the inspector saw that the guards posted on the perimeter kept a watchful eye on the surroundings. Inspector Hari concluded that it was exceedingly difficult for anyone to pass without being noticed and it would be a herculean task to lay siege on the place.

The SUV entered the barbed fence surrounding the warehouse after it was checked thoroughly a second time and stopped before the entrance of the warehouse. The big steel shutters lifted to allow the SUV to enter inside the warehouse. Inspector Hari saw men armed with sub machine guns approach the SUV and after clarifying with the driver about the passenger allowed him to disembark from the vehicle. The inspector saw that the entire operation was conducted with military precision.

The driver signaled the inspector to follow him to the next room where he found the reason for his journey waiting for him. The nude girls were made to stand in a line for the inspection and the inspector checked their faces as he passed them. Some tried to cover their bodies with their hands and avoided looking at him, some looked at him with scorn and some cried loudly covering their faces. After examining them thoroughly, he sighed with satisfaction.

Is this everyone cried the inspector? Did you miss anyone?

The leader shook his head. 200 girls were brought inside the warehouse from all over India and they are standing before you. If you have any concerns, feel free to contact our boss.

Inspector Hari hurriedly dialed the minister's number.

Sir, they aren't here.

Are you sure barked the minister?

Yes.

The minister laughed loudly.

That Narayan bastard almost led me to believe that we would find our girls there. I sent you just to make sure that they weren't there even though I trust our comrades. That nincompoop still couldn't find the bastard who had actually kidnapped our children. The first thing I am going to do is to strip his badge and throw him in the gutters because he wasted a lot of our time by making us suspect our partners in crime.

Sir, the minister's secretary interrupted.

I told you specifically not to disturb me, you idiot. Now make yourself scarce before I lose my temper.

The minister shouted at his secretary.

But Sir, Mr. Narayanan Kutty found both the girls, your granddaughter as well as the inspector's daughter. They are being kept under observation in the Government hospital but it seems that they were unharmed. Mr. Narayanan Kutty is waiting outside to convey the good news.

What? Shouted the minister. Send him in immediately.

The minister again resumed the conversation with Inspector Hari.

Good news at last, he shouted excitedly.

I heard the conversation; Inspector Hari told the minister. I will catch the next flight to Coimbatore and on second thought I have decided to check the girls again a little more thoroughly. I may have missed something the first time.

The inspector looked at the naked girls with lust as he spoke.

You slimy bastard. Bear in mind that the goods are not to be tampered with. Can you describe them for me. The minister asked ardently.

Suddenly the whole place was in a state of turmoil as the guardians of the warehouse scampered like ants. Inspector Hari could hear the familiar noises of the rotors of helicopters hovering the warehouse and saw men in camouflages appear in from every direction. After a prolonged skirmish, the guardians of the warehouse were finally subdued. The kidnapped girls were safely rescued by the police and Inspector Hari was arrested along with the smugglers.

In the next few days, many important people occupying high positions in the Government were put behind bars. The leader of the smuggling ring, Tara Singh was arrested along with his subordinate when they tried to leave the country.

The newspapers screamed the success of the sting operation orchestrated by Mr. Narayanan Kutty to capture the smugglers and expose the network. They also praised the efforts of the Joint police force from different states of India who took part in the operation. A list of the people involved in the smuggling, that included the crème de la crème of the society was displayed in every channel.

A week after the arrests, Narayanan Kutty stood before the commissioner of Coimbatore city.

Well done Mr. Narayanan Kutty, for disrupting the network of child kidnappers in India and exposing the puppet heads behind those kidnappings. You are really a whiz in solving the cases.

Narayanan Kutty shook his head.

Sir, I may have helped catch the smuggling ring and its leaders but there are still other networks that are yet to be uncovered.

The police commissioner agreed.

One at a time, Mr. Narayanan Kutty. Be proud that you had saved a lot of girls. Now why do you look so forlorn despite your accomplishments?

I don't deserve the full credit for the operation, sir.

Ah! Teamwork, is it? I didn't know that modesty was one of your qualities. Still, you led the entire operation and deserve my utmost respect.

But I didn't solve the case of the two missing girls, Narayanan Kutty continued.

Were they not safely returned to their parents with not one scratch on their bodies asked the commissioner? Didn't you find who kidnapped them?

Narayana Kutty shook his head.

No sir and I don't intend to.

The commissioner looked at him strangely and asked.

Is there any reason behind your benevolence.

Sir, Narayana Kutty continued. Please don't judge me but without him, the person who had kidnapped the children of the minister and the Inspector, it would not have been possible to catch the smuggling ring. Without his valuable information at the right time, all the girls would be satisfying the hunger of some rich maniac.

Do you wish to elaborate on that? Asked the commissioner.

In the beginning, I suspected that minister's granddaughter and the inspector's daughter were kidnapped by the smuggling network. But as I started to dig deeply, I discovered that both the minister and the Inspector were part of the network, which proved that the kidnapper's intention was far from nefarious and he knew their involvement in the network. It didn't make any sense to assume that the smugglers kidnapped the children of the minister and the inspector who were part of the network. So, it became clear to me that the two girls were kidnapped by someone who held a grudge against the minister and the inspector.

When did you come to this conclusion? Asked the commissioner.

Mr. Narayanan Kutty continued that after receiving a tip he investigated the minister and the inspector secretly by tapping their mobile phones and tailing them using plains clothed detectives. By doing so, he had unearthed the network operating in Tamil Nadu but still he had to find the location of the warehouse.

So, you played a ruse on the minister making him believe that his granddaughter was kidnapped by Tara Singh's network and sent a squad to follow the inspector to find the secret lair and orchestrated a successful sting operation on the warehouse by coordinating with the Maharashtra State police and the paramilitary. The ploy worked superbly and you managed to flush out the network.

Narayanan Kutty nodded as the commissioner spoke.

But you had already submitted a detailed report which included all the things you have said, the commissioner continued.

But Sir, Narayanan Kutty hesitated. There are some things that I neglected to mention. The real mastermind behind the operation is the one who kidnapped the children of the minister and the inspector and he was the informer who helped me to connect both the cases. Also, he had inside knowledge of the police department, the corrupt officers manning the check posts, and knew about the Joint hands club's activities. He executed the kidnapping perfectly so that anyone would conclude that the two girls were grabbed by the smugglers. The minister and the inspector were misled by this ruse and we managed to nail them.

Do you have any evidence to support this? Asked the commissioner.

No sir, Mr. Narayanan Kutty answered. It is just a hunch.

Narayanan Kutty left the commissioner office and let out a sigh. He felt relieved somehow by sharing some of his revelations with somebody.

Where to Sir?

The old driver asked Narayana Kutty his destination.

The airport he said simply. I am going home.

At the airport, Narayanan Kutty turned to the driver and saluted him.

Sir cried the old man. I am supposed to salute you.

Narayanan Kutty smiled and left.

The old police officer, the same officer who had felt pity for the couple that cried before the station a few days back looked into his glove compartment.

An old newspaper clipping was visible which said

'12-year daughter of a police constable still missing'.

The photo of a girl with her parents was seen under it. The father looked like the younger version of the old police officer.

RAINDROP 6

Great dreams of great dreamers are always transcended.

A. P. J. Abdul Kalam

Soothsaying radio

A village near Thanjavur

Vande Mataram! Vande Mataram!

Jai Hind! Jai Hind!

Bharat Matha ki jay!

These words were repeated by millions of Indians when the British decided to give its long-sought freedom. After a long time under the rule of an outsider, the people would be governed by Indians and their brothers. People waited anxiously till the Indian flag was raised high and inhaled their first breath of freedom. Some ran madly in the streets as if they had grown new legs and were running for the first time in their lives. Some shouted with all their might at the few British who were leaving to their homeland, declaring that they were no more slaves. Some pinched themselves to see that they were not in some dreamland.

People cheered at their leaders asking the people to join hands in building a great nation, even greater than the British, even greater than Germany, and even greater than the United States of America. Everyone believed their words and dreamt of becoming prosperous.

No more poverty, they thought.

No more violence they thought.

No more slavery they thought.

No more illiteracy they thought.

No more racism they thought.

The air smells fresh and the water tastes more delicious said the poets about free India.

Eighteen years after the people of Sudhandirapuram near Thanjavur worked in the same fields as they did for many generations, ate the same food, drank the same water, and faced the same poverty.

Some youngsters asked the village elders about why things were still the same after eighteen years of independence, why they had to work for meager wages and why they were still eating once or twice a day, sometimes go to bed with empty stomachs.

After a long thought, one of the elders spoke.

Listen, children, we are a long way from Delhi where the Indians raised the flag of freedom and the winds of independence still didn't reach us because it has to blow over thousands of kilometers.

Then how come the songs played from Delhi reach us through the All India Radio asked one mischievous youth.

The old man smiled.

Because the All India Radio started to operate years before our India got its freedom.

The skinny boy in ragged clothes was sitting on the roof of his hut at the edge of his village, playing a rustic single-stringed musical instrument, the Kudukku Vina, and thought that the birds flew in the air following his rhythm. He saw a flash from the corner of his eye and stood up looking at the distant horizon where few rain clouds had gathered.

Was it lightning? he wondered.

Another flash streaked across the sky followed by the sound of distant thunder.

He slid to the ground and ran towards the Panchayat tree where everyone had gathered for the arrival of the village president.

It is going to rain he shouted. I saw lightning and I heard thunder.

The boy ran through the crowd repeating this till he reached the elder.

Are you sure? He asked the boy.

The villagers looked at him with pessimism as he had done the same thing many times before.

We thought the rains would be plentiful in free India but it is still waiting for the winds of freedom to blow from the North said, someone.

Everyone waited for the rain but was sorely disappointed when it didn't rain.

The village president had gone to the town to meet the collector to submit the pleas of the village for better roads, and access to public transport.

It was late when he returned so he asked everyone to assemble before his house to listen to news broadcasted by the AIR. It was the new routine of the village since the new radio was installed in the President's house.

The president sat in his usual rocking chair and his family was sitting on a mat made of reeds near his side on a platform in front of his big house while the others sat on the ground. The radio was kept in the front room of the house and everyone could see it through the big windows.

They waited for the end of the news. They didn't care about the events in other parts of the world, about the economic policies of the government, or the fashion trends of Indian celebrities.

They were waiting for the weather report. They were waiting for the news of good rains that year. But they only heard disappointment.

The monsoon has again failed in India for the consecutive year and it is expected that India would receive lesser than usual rains this monsoon. The government has warned the farmers to delay their sowing till later and requests the fellow citizens to pray for the rain.

A dead silence followed by the anguished cries of the poor farmers reverberated through the village.

I had lost an entire crop last year and was hoping to recuperate the losses this year, but if the rains fail, I will be hanging on the big tamarind tree outside our village cried a farmer.

I had hoped to send my son to the city for his higher studies cried a farmer.

I had hoped to make some jewels for my daughter's marriage cried another.

I had hoped to settle my debts to the moneylender, someone cried.

Some beat their chests and raised their hands towards the sky pleading to the rain God. Some talked with the Panchayat President, hoping for any solution to the problem. The poorest of the poor farmers abandoned hope and sat on the ground with hands on their heads.

An old woman, with long white hair matted in strands, walked slowly in front of the crowd. Everyone looked at the village soothsayer with respect. Some fell on her feet and asked her the reason for their woes. The old woman in a red sari and a large round Kumkum mark on her forehead spat the juiced of the tobacco leaf on the ground and raised her hands

The Gods have forsaken us again, cried the village soothsayer. Our mother, Ellaiamman has cursed us and demands blood sacrifice. We must perform many rituals to appease her. A virgin girl must be chosen and she should walk around the village naked. A large pyre must be constructed and the village women must cover their bodies with Neem leaves and walk on the hot ashes. Each household must bring a goat or a cock and sacrifice it at the altar before God to quench her thirst.

The old soothsayer spoke with such ferocity that the people prayed to her with fear. They believed that God had descended into her body and spoke through her mouth. The president announced that he would make sure that her instructions would be followed meticulously.

The date of the ritual was finalized and the villagers were prohibited to leave the village till the rituals were completed. In the next few days, the village looked beautiful with its streets painted with beautiful kolams, little flags tied between posts fluttered in the breeze, and bunches of neem leaves, and yellow flowers decorated the houses. The faces of the villagers were grim but they had not lost their hopes.

A virgin girl was chosen, the 13-year-old Kamala, who lived with her grandmother in a small hut. She was taken to the president's house and was treated like royalty since her sacrifice would bring the rains. A spacious room was allocated to her and the ladies of the house served her. The poor girl who had lived with poverty all her life and was ignored by everyone found herself surrounded by luxuries. She tasted delicious foods, wore beautiful clothes, and was treated with respect by everyone including the president.

Her most favorite pastime was listening to the radio. She was fascinated by the sounds; the voices and music emerging from the box and listened to it with rapt attention. Soon it became an obsession such that she crept into the room where the radio was kept and spent many sleepless nights staring at the radio.

Tragedy struck when she was found dead by the president's wife hugging the radio and the people of the village considered it as a bad omen. The soothsayer said that God had punished her and her body must be burned immediately. She was cremated without an inquiry and another girl was chosen to replace her.

The village soothsayer blamed the villagers for not choosing a virgin girl for the ritual and people threw abuses at her grandmother for not raising her properly.

On a ritual day, many animals were slaughtered on the sacrificial altar. Women covered their bodies with leaves of the neem tree and ran over the burning cinders and shouting God's name loudly. Men covered their bodies with turmeric paste and pierced little tridents resembling God's weapon in their cheeks till it came out from the other cheek. As the night approached, the women forced the shy virgin girl to remove her clothes and sent her on her journey around the village. In the end, the soothsayer stood before the village, her body trembling and her hands rose towards the deity.

Listen she shouted; her voice rang silencing the crowd. You are fools and sinners she continued. Did you think that I would not know about your misdeeds? Did you think that I will not punish you severely? You will all repent for your mistakes. She shook her entire body after shouting these words.

The villagers looked at the soothsayer with fear. The women ululated loudly in a high pitch to calm the God Ellaiamman who had taken possession of the soothsayer's body and spoke to them.

The soothsayer's assistant shouted.

Please forgive your children, Kind mother. You are our only salvation. Please tell us what to do to appease you. Put aside your anger before it burns us and calm down mother.

The soothsayer shouted some more abuses and narrated a set of instructions. She finally pardoned them.

The crowd shouted in unison.

Please bless us with abundant rains this year and tell us when to plant the crops.

You can start planting as usual and you will get copious rainfall if you followed my instructions properly.

A pot of water mixed with turmeric was poured on the soothsayer and she came out of her trance as the yellow water trickled down her body.

The crowd sighed with relief and dispersed. The soothsayer's assistants collected the offerings of food, money, and Arak liquor left by the villagers. The inebriated soothsayer was carried to her dwelling.

The villagers started to plow their fields to prepare them for planting and ignored the warnings issued by the government to postpone the plantation. They also didn't bother to assemble at the President's house to hear the weather report.

The President switched on the radio and waited for the familiar voice of the news reporter but he could hear only static noise. The static noise didn't clear even after adjusting the frequency and the few who had assembled started to leave. As he was about to turn off the radio, the noise cleared and a girl's voice was heard.

It warned the people to delay planting the crops for a month since the monsoon was delayed. The villagers were surprised by the voice of a young girl instead of the usual weatherman. Maybe they are broadcasting a new program they thought. The girl's voice retold the warnings several times and the radio went silent.

The next day a huge crowd gathered before the president's house, hearing about the strange girl's voice and most of them were skeptical came just to hear the voice with their ears.

Good evening, my dear people of Sudhandhirapuram continued the girl's voice at the same time as yesterday. You have been good to me and I can't blame you for the sins of a few people. So, I will help you in this difficult period. But I promise that the crime against me would not go unpunished. Don't plant the crops till I tell you so and heed my warning if you want to reap a good harvest. The village soothsayer would spit blood tomorrow and die wailing in pain before the whole village. I hope that you will believe me after this.

After relaying its message, the radio turned off by itself and didn't work after many futile attempts.

The news spread like wildfire through the village.

People gathered in groups and spoke in hushed tones about the girl on the radio predicting the imminent death of the soothsayer whom they worshipped. They talked about the mysterious death of the young Kamala in the president's house and the president's decision not to investigate it further.

Conspiracy rumors spread among the youngsters who blamed the inefficient president and their ignorant and superstitious elders who believed every word spoken by the village soothsayer.

To put an end to the rumors, the president announced that all the people of the village should assemble before the huge peepal tree where the elders of the village would conduct the weekly Panchayat. The Panchayat was like the equivalent of a judicial court where people brought their grievances and sought justice.

The villagers waited before the small platform before the peepal tree the next day for the arrival of the jury. The president arrived with the other elders; they were the judges and their word is final. They sat on the platform and began the day's proceedings.

They advised the villagers to refrain from spreading rumors and warned the youngsters to stop their blasphemy against the soothsayer. They called the soothsayer before the Panchayat to prove that she was healthy. The soothsayer stood before the people with her assistants carrying burning camphor in her palm. She deplored the villager for their breach of trust in her and their elders and cursed them for their sins. After a long time, uttering curses, she was advised by the elders to retire to her house and ended the Panchayat. As the villagers were about to disperse, the soothsayer let out a scream and fell on the ground writhing in pain.

The villagers witnessed the first prediction of the girl in the video come true as the soothsayer died with blood gushing from her mouth, her eyes bulging and her body twisted like a twine before the village.

It is just a coincidence said the elder and the village medic who checked the body of the soothsayer. She died of a stroke and natural causes because of her heavy drinking, he proclaimed his diagnosis. Not because some girl cursed her.

Half the village believed him but the other half who were superstitious believed the words of the girl on the radio.

A huge crowd gathered before the president's house as usual in the evening and waited for the girl's voice.

The radio came alive and the childish voice spoke again.

Good evening my brethren it said. Please don't mourn for the death of the fraudulent soothsayer who was cheating you for a long time making false predictions and swindling you even at this difficult period at the same time gorging on the food and the liquor offered to God.

It paused for a while letting the people speak to each other.

A great calamity awaits the president's family in the coming week. The president's son will go to jail and the president will not be alive said the voice. The radio died after conveying its message.

A great uproar rose from the crowd.

The president stood angrily and hit the radio with his slippers.

The damn machine is broken he cried hysterically at the villagers and ordered his servants to close the windows. The villagers expressed their sympathies to the compassionate president's wife and left to their homes.

The radio was not displayed for a week and it also didn't turn on.

In the following week, the long-unsolved mystery of the disappearance of the temple jewels in the town where the president was a trustee was finally resolved. The police found the jewels buried in the grounds of the rice mill belonging to the village president and the news reached that they would soon arrive to arrest the president and his son, the main culprits of the theft.

To save his face, the president hung himself in the same room where he kept his radio and his son surrendered to the police. The villagers saw the president's body hanging with his tongue out and the radio sitting silently near him, the only eyewitness to his death.

Soon the news of the miraculous radio traveled to other villages and many arrived in their bullock carts to see it. Hearing the requests of the villagers, the grieving yet noble president's wife decided to allow the people to see the radio.

A bigger crowd than ever gathered before the president's house.

The people from different villages waited anxiously for the girl's voice and they were not disappointed.

The girl's voice was heard again after more than a week greeting the people.

Good evening to my fellow villagers of Sudhandhirapuram and others from the nearby villagers. The crowd cheered.

As I said before, please refrain from planting your crops till next month. The monsoon rains will soon arrive by the blessings of our God, Ellaiamman and you will again prosper. The recent deaths of the soothsayer, the president, and his son were a necessity and they paid with their lives for their crimes against me. Erase their memories from their minds and work hard preparing your fields before the rains.

The radio became silent.

The people waited for the girl to speak again for a long time, but it didn't speak again for a month. The people never stopped coming to hear their beloved voice of the girl on the radio The radio was decorated with flowers and treated like a deity. The radio room was converted into a small shrine.

After a month, the radio switched on and the crowd cheered when the girl's voice came alive. It advised the villagers to start their planting tomorrow.

The actual weather report heard in other villages was that the monsoon had failed and only a few areas would receive below the average rainfall for a few days. It also requested the farmers to refrain from planting the crops that needed copious water and advised them to plant the drought-resistant varieties.

Except for the villagers of Sudhandhirapuram, everyone followed the advice of the weather report and didn't tend to their fields. The crowd kept gathering before the radio and waited for the girl's voice advising them to plant the crops every day.

It became hotter in the following days and dry winds blew dirt over the villages. Everyone made fun of the villagers of Sudhandhirapuram who had trusted their radio instead of the news and planted their crops. All the signs showed that it would be a very dry season, but the villagers were headstrong in their faith in the radio girl.

Soon the news reached the village of Sudhandhirapuram that depression had appeared in the Bay of Bengal and was proceeding fast towards the Indian subcontinent. The people of Sudhandhirapuram cheered and the others looked at them with envy.

In the following days, the storm weakened and was expected to proceed towards northern India. But again, it strengthened and was proceeding towards Kerala. It played games in the next few days, and the moods of the people kept cycling between happiness and sorrow.

The good news came finally that the storm would cross the shore and many regions in southern India would receive heavy rainfall for a week. The villagers of Sudhandhirauram gathered before the president's house watched the rain clouds gather in the distant horizon and heard the thunder rumbling.

The radio spoke again when the first raindrops fell on the villagers.

Good evening said the voice. The rains have finally arrived as I promised. Now it's time to reveal a secret. The girl named Kamala who was supposed to bring the rain was raped and killed by the President's son and the president with the soothsayer's help hid the truth of her murder. You believed the soothsayer's words and abused her. But I am not angry with the people who had provided food for my family in tough times, who had helped my grandmother when she was sick, and treated me like royalty when I was selected as the chosen one. I had waited long enough and now will seek the great beyond. Don't forget me, Now I must say Goodbye.

Tears welled in every face gathered before the house. The children stopped their play and clung to their parents. The dogs howled, the cows mooed and the goats bleated. The birds on the branches of the huge Peepal tree scattered from their resting places chirping loudly and flew away.

The village mourned for the girl on the radio and the people pleaded with the girl to not leave them.

Only the rains could bring them happiness as the raindrops washed away the tears from their eyes.

RAINDROP 7

You know, Willie Wonka said it best: we are the makers of dreams, the dreamers of dreams.

Herb Brooks

Kanka's dog across the rainbow bridge

Sandra. Where are you, my princess?

Sandra dear, come to dada.

Charles called his 10-year-old daughter with love.

I must present her with the best gift, whatever she wishes for her birthday. I will be the best dad in the world.

Charles thought about celebrating his child's birthday grandly.

I have a week to plan her birthday and it should be a memorable day in her life. What should I purchase for her? Maybe A Barbie doll?

Charles was still deep in his thoughts when Sandra rushed towards and hugged him.

Yes, dada. She laughed.

What would you like for your birthday, dear?

Sandra hesitated.

Dada, she said and paused.

I want a puppy for my birthday.

A puppy, is it? Are you sure you will take care of it?

Sandra nodded with a big smile.

One of my friends' imports dogs from abroad. His kennel has many high-breed dog pups, so we will visit his place and select one for you.

But dada, Sandra said and hesitated.

What is it, Sandra? Charles asked expecting some weird request from his daughter.

Every time before his daughter asked something which he didn't approve of, she would fidget, her lips would quiver and she would stutter. Charles saw that she exhibited all the signs now. It was as if she knew that he would not like her request and as if she knew his mind. A 10-year-old kid judging me, he thought and dismissed the thought.

Come on Sandra. You know that Dada always gives you the best in the world.

But dada, a dog had given birth to a litter of pups behind our garden. One of the pups strayed inside our garden. I gave her food and she was incredibly happy. She follows me around and barks at me to play with her. Can we keep it?

Sandra told her dad knowing that he would not agree but she anyway tried her best.

Come here Sandra and sit on dad's lap.

Sandra knew that her dad was going to deny her request by making some excuses.

Sandra, Dada always gives the best gifts to you. We can go to my friend's kennel and see the puppies which are well maintained and trained by professionals. I can't allow a stray dog and a mongrel from the streets into my house. Only God knows how many diseases it may carry in its body. And they would wreak havoc in the house. What will our neighbors think of us? We live in a posh locality and we would be the laughing stock of the neighborhood if we bring a stray dog into our house.

Sandra listened to her dad's long lecture and sighed.

But daddy, I will clean the dog and train it myself. Once it is within our walls, it will no longer be a stray dog. Sandra pleaded to her dad.

A Street dog is still a mongrel no matter where it is kept. I want only the best, Sandra. As I said I will take you to....

But dada, Sandra interrupted. When we attended the sermon in the church last week, the pastor said that God embraces not the beautiful or the cleverest creatures but the weak ones who had strayed from its path. Surely, He would want us to prefer the street dog over the high breed dog.

Charles was fascinated with his daughter's clever reply at the same time irritated that she preferred a dirty mongrel.

Let's go to my friend's kennel first, and no Buts he said when Sandra tried to interrupt him.

Charles Desouza lived with his wife and daughter in a big four-bedroom villa with all the comforts that could be found in a rich man's house. It had a big garden in the back and a tennis court. A beautiful lawn with a small swing and a swimming pool occupied the front. Behind his house was a slum where the poorest of the society lived with their families. Sandra would often wonder if they were the happiest because many children ran around laughing and playing with others covered by dirty clothes dotted with a thousand holes. She would compare them with her rich neighbors, who were always polite, walked with their heads held high, and complained about everything in the world while the poor who lived at the back led carefree lives.

Charles was born with a silver spoon and preferred to fill his house with the top brands. His wardrobe was filled with shirts from Armani, perfumes from Bulgari and he made sure that his family also used only the top brands. He preferred to mingle with only his rich friends and looked at others with disgust.

Sandra accompanied her dad to the big kennel belonging to her father's friend and looked at the beautiful pups in the cages. Some looked at her with drooping eyes, some barked at her with excitement, some wagged their tails and tried to lick her hand and some lifted their heads, yawned, and went back to sleep. She could hear her dad asking his friend what he wanted was the best.

At last, she chose a pup with large drooping ears and round eyes.

Excellent choice said her dad's friend.

Is it the best asked Charles?

It is a Cavalier King Charles spaniel my friend and it was preferred as a pet by the royal families in England. It is the aristocrat of dogs and you can find it in paintings drawn by famous artists. He is named after the King Charles of England so it says everything about itself.

Charles smiled. Name your price.

The pup that had strayed in was given to the servant and the high breed dog became a member of the DeSouza family.

Six months passed in a jiffy.

Sandra loved the pup and took care of it with love. She did everything from taking it on long walks to bathing it. Charles bragged about the dog to his neighbors. Soon some of the other rich had also bought pups of the same breed.

His next-door neighbor, Vasanth had asked him about the dog and immediately Charles explained to him about its royal ancestry and that it was awfully expensive.

What about the dog you keep in the garden he asked. He disturbs everyone with his howling at night and shits everywhere on the street. Some of the other neighbors complained that it had been tearing their garbage bags. We thought that it came from the slums at the back. After a long time, Mrs. Geetha, your other neighbor found the mongrel inside your house when she was tending to her exotic plants in her garden.

I didn't know that you will keep a mongrel in your house. Vasanth asked him mockingly.

Charles's nostrils flared.

There is no such dog in our house, he shouted. I had complained about a street dog that keeps sitting near the front gate, barks when I go outside, and even follows me every morning during my walks. I am the victim here as the dog is hell-bent on disturbing my peace and the association did nothing about it.

The association responded to your complaints and brought the dog catchers. They caught a couple of dogs but not the mongrel dog which terrorized this neighborhood because she ran inside your house.

He entered his house and called everyone.

He looked at his wife. Please tell me we are not sheltering a street dog.

Everyone looked at him with fear.

After a long silence, Mrs. Clara spoke.

I am sorry Charles, his wife Clara said. Do you remember the pup which had strayed into our garden a long time ago and Sandra asked your permission to keep her?

Yes, I remember said, Charles. Don't tell me it's the same bloody dog.

Our servant took it to her house but the pup didn't stay there for long and it returned to our home. No matter how many times we tried to send it away, it kept on coming back. Sandra also liked it very much and I think the dog wants to be a part of our family.

Charles exploded.

You have brought me nothing but shame by giving me a mongrel place in our house. After expressing clearly, that I want it thrown out, you went behind my back. What will our neighbors think of me? I will be the laughing stock of this neighborhood and everyone will look down at me from now. I want that dog, gone by today evening, or else I am going to kill it myself.

Forget about our neighbors with their loud mouths. Rocky loves you very much, Charles said his wife, Clara. I still don't know why. You hate the dog with all your heart but Rocky wants to be your pet. Whenever you go for your early morning walks, he follows you diligently a few steps behind you to ensure your safety. When you come home every day, he welcomes you with his barking and we would know that you had arrived.

Few weeks before he was incessantly barking at something in our garden and we found that it was pointing at a snake. It was hiding in the bushes, Sandra's favorite place in the garden. If it wasn't for Rocky, imagine what would have happened to our child. I beg you to ignore our foolish neighbors and accept Rocky as one of our family.

No. Charles shouted at the top of his voice. I would not accept any excuses.

His phone rang. Charles took it out with anger, looked at the caller id, and calmed down. After speaking for a long time, he returned.

I must visit one of our factories to take care of some issues so I will be away for a few days. I must leave immediately to reach there before it gets dark.

And one more thing he continued. Make sure to remove the stray dog from my house today and when I return, I should not find it loitering before our house.

He took his car outside and found the stray dog wagging its tail at him. He closed the gates and found it still wagging at him from a distance. He watched it for a long time. The innocent dog thought that he was being friendly walked towards him with his tongue sticking out. Charles saw Vasant glaring at him from his house and his neighbor, Mrs. Geetha was entering her house looking at him with disgust.

The first raindrops fell on him.

He quickly got inside his car and watched the dog coming next to the car as it started to rain heavily. As he started his car, he felt the whole neighborhood watching him and gossiping about him. He fought a wave of nausea and saw the dog had put its front paws on the car watching him through the window. The bloody dog wants to get into my costly car, he thought. He pressed the accelerator and turned the steering wheel to the left. He sped away with satisfaction when the dog's leg caught under one of the car's rear wheels. The last thing he heard was a loud mournful howl.

Charles returned to his house after a couple of days and found that the stray dog had disappeared. It was not in its usual place.

The servant opened the door and he entered the house with satisfaction. Maybe he was dead when he ran it over or his wife had the good sense to finally get rid of it. He found the house unusually silent. His wife and child were not at home. Every time he returned home, Sandra would come running towards him and jump at him shouting with joy. His wife would not be far behind and would smile at the father and daughter duo laughing with happiness.

Where is everyone, he asked the servant.

Sir, Clara madam is in the kitchen and little Sandra is in her bedroom studying for her exams.

Since when she started studying by herself, Charles wondered as he went to her room. Sandra didn't come to him running.

Hi, dada she said and returned to her books.

She is probably sulking; Charles thought and went to the kitchen. His wife looked at him coldly and asked him whether he had eaten.

Did you do what you were supposed to do?

Clara looked away.

Charles continued shaking his head.

I did it for the good of this family and now I am being treated as the villain.

Charles sighed.

You must make your child understand these trivial things.

What trivial things, Clara responded angrily. What can I say to a 10-year-old girl who watched her dad trying to kill a dog because it was not worth it? We watched everything from the balcony. We watched you glare at Rocky and get inside the car. We watched you run over the dog intentionally. Didn't you have the heart to look back at your handiwork? Were you happy that you hurt an innocent soul and restored the good name to this family?

Stop your bickering, foolish bitch he shouted and left the house.

Charles returned late in the night drunk and was let in by the servant.

Where are my loyal wife and my loving kid he shouted? I have given them everything and they respond with disloyalty. Where is the fucking dog?

The servant withdrew to her room silently.

He carried a bottle of beer and a food parcel to the garden as he did every weekend. Sitting comfortably in his usual chair, he drank the beer and ate the chicken lollipop. He threw the half-eaten pieces into the bushes as he usually did and saw a shadow cross near him. It was the mongrel limping in three legs towards the bushes. With an angry bellow, he took a big stick and ran towards the dog. He stumbled on a rock and fell on the ground hitting his head hard on the process.

He woke up with a severe headache on a hospital bed with his head wrapped tightly and his wife in deep sleep while sitting in a chair near his bed. His daughter was sleeping on the couch hugging tightly her favorite doll. Sensing him, Clara woke up and asked whether he was alright.

She said that he had fallen and hit his head hard on the ground. When they found him, he was lying in a pool of blood. He had lost a lot of blood and was in the ICU for two days, but luckily there were no major injuries.

He remembered the night.

If it wasn't for the damn dog, I would not be lying in this bed.

Charles said with fury.

Clara gripped his shoulders.

If it wasn't for Rocky, you would be dead, she shouted.

Rocky's hind leg was squashed when you ran over him and we had to rush him to the veterinarian. But he couldn't save his leg because it was in shambles and amputated it. But it didn't hate you even after that. You were lying in the garden with a stone clutched tightly in your hand and we realized that you fell chasing Rocky.

We were woken by Rocky's loud barks and howls in the middle of the night and it led to you lying in the bushes. If it weren't for Rocky, we would never have found you. The doctors said that if we had brought you a little later, he would not have been able to save you. I would have lost my husband and Sandra would have lost her father. But thanks to dear God, Rocky was sent as a guardian angel to save you.

Charles didn't speak about the dog again till he was discharged and was on the way to his house.

Where is the dog? He asked his wife.

Don't worry, said Clara. I had sent it to my friend's animal shelter and it won't bother you again.

Charles said nothing.

Charles had not recovered fully so the doctors advised Clara to take diligent care of him and warned her to keep his head dry for a couple of days.

Clara woke up the next day late in the morning and found the vacant bed. She had stayed late the previous night because Charles was running a fever. Maybe he is with Sandra; she thought and walked to her daughter's room. Sandra was watching her favorite cartoon show.

Did you see daddy? Clara asked.

No. I thought he was with you.

Clara searched the entire house and didn't find him. Charles's car was there so he could not have left without it. Where did he go? She wondered.

She heard a car horn and watched a taxi pull up before her house. It was raining so heavily that she couldn't identify the person getting down from the vehicle. As the figure opened the gate, the excited bark of a dog pricked her ears.

Was it rocky? She thought.

Charles approached her completely soaked in the rain carrying the dog in his hands. He laughed as Rocky kept licking his face.

Damn dog wants to give me a facial, he shouted.

Clara raised her eyebrows and looked at him.

Why Charles? Did you bring him because he saved you?

No Charles said. I brought him because he helped me find my heart.

And because he is family he said to his wife.

Clara looked at the rain falling heavily.

Maybe it washed away his pride, she thought.

RAINDROP 8

I dreamed I was a butterfly,
flitting around in the sky; then I awoke.
Now I wonder: Am I a man who dreamt of being a
butterfly, or am I a butterfly dreaming that
I am a man?

Zhuangzi

An alternate world

Hey! you! What are you doing there? A deep male voice rang through my ears. I looked around to see that I was standing on train tracks and some people were watching me from the platform. My vision was a little blurred so I could see only their shadows.

Get out of there shouted the figure with the deep voice.

I heard the loud sound of the train's horn behind me and the familiar grating noise of its wheels rolling on the tracks moving towards me.

How did I end up here and why can't I make a decision. Is that a train about to crush me?

You, weak loser cried the voice. Take my hand if you want to live.

My hands felt like lead.

Only the fear of the train crushing my body gave me the strength to move my hand. I raised my hands towards the voice using all my strength.

Little more shouted the voice. Can't you move faster?

Suddenly I was pulled from the tracks and thrown on the hard platform as the train thundered past me.

Thank you, Sir.

Don't make me blush, the voice said mockingly. Already my wives look at you with jealousy. You are incredibly lucky that we were passing through this station where no trains stop. What's your pathetic story and why are you dressed like a man?

Slowly my vision cleared. By their rustic voices, I could understand that they were simple village folk. A half-nude woman wearing a dhoti and a towel around her neck watched me with amusement and three men covered in a sari-like dress sat near him looking at me with shock.

She is a foreigner said one of the men in a feminine voice.

Hey, why are you looking at my husband instead of answering him? The woman is not right in the head. Look at her staring with those empty eyes.

I didn't know how to react and I didn't know what to speak. A female spoke in a deep masculine voice, pulled me up, and introduced me to her male wives. My head was spinning.

Two of the males had a pouch like a kangaroo on their bodies and I could see babies poking out from them. The third one had a smaller pouch but his back bulged under her clothes.

I am Momed, introduced the woman and these are my wives.

They are my babies. My first wife produced five and my second produced six. My third wife may give me seven by the look of her number of sacs. But these things can't be predicted. Why don't you dress like a woman because if you go out like this you may be violated?

Still dazed, I looked at my clothes. I had worn a t-shirt and khaki shorts.

I am Ulla. What's wrong with my dress? I asked Momed.

You show too much of your body. You don't cover your head with a veil.

Momed replied with a smile.

We walked for a while through empty streets and waited near a bus stop.

Sir, what is this place? I hail from the city Abi, and my father is one of the richest in the city. If you guide me to my father, I will make sure that you will be generously rewarded for your service.

What's your father's name? She asked

Uddhin I answered.

Well, Ulla daughter of Uddhin. We are also traveling to Abi seeking employment. Maybe you can travel with us. We will take the bus to Abi. Do you have any money? Momed asked

I put my hands inside my pockets and took out a piece of paper with the single word "Repent" written on it.

The daughter of a rich man doesn't have a penny said one of her wives, the males.

It's alright ladies as long as I get paid. Now cover your faces and shut your mouths because I see the bus.

The bus stopped and Momed went inside followed by the three males. I saw the occupants dressed similarly, the men dressed in veiled saris, and the women mostly topless and a dhoti. Even the bus driver was a half-nude female.

Are you coming or not, shouted the bus driver in her hoarse voice. I climbed the steps and heard the women shouting like wolves. I saw them looking at me with their mouths open and as I passed them several hands pinched my butt. I winced in pain and sat in a vacant seat. Immediately a half-nude woman sat next to me, her hands around my neck. She was drunk and her alcoholic breath made me nauseous as she turned to speak to me.

Lady, why don't you sit on my lap? I pushed her away but she kept falling on me as the bus made its journey towards Abi. Her hands kept groping my body and I felt my blood boil to see her boobs pressing against me. I responded by pressing her boobs which made her grunt with satisfaction. She pulled my face and kissed me, her long tongue swirling inside my mouth. She pulled my hands between her legs.

One of Momed's wives shouted at me.

What are you doing? Do you want to give birth to a bunch of bastards? Look at you copulate with a stranger shamelessly in public.

Momed came and pushed the women away.

You are a slut. She shouted at me. I don't care what you do after I deliver you to your father but until then you must obey me.

I heard many voices telling me that I was a slut and needed to be punished.

Look at her dress said, someone. She is trying to seduce the men. Maybe she is a prostitute.

If she travels in this dress, she will get raped.

And dumped in the river

Serves her right for wearing such a dress said another.

What's wrong with my dress? I felt like shouting at them but was too embarrassed.

The bus reached the outskirts of a big city and I saw large billboards with pictures of beautiful men dressed like me. I realized that they were models promoting the brands.

Did I land in an alien world, I thought. Maybe this is hell and I am being punished for my sins. I recollected my past as the bus entered the city.

I was the son of a rich merchant in the city of Jewels, the Abi which was the envy of the world. The city of Abi had more millionaires than anywhere else in the world and its rich inhabitants were known for their luxurious lifestyles. People drove inexpensive cars, owned private jets and boats, married many wives, and lived extravagantly.

I was the eldest son of my father's twenty children from five wives and the heir to his riches. I lived in abundance since I was born and always had my way. I owned many cars and houses including the ones in other countries. My country had strict rules about women and other things. Even when the world stepped into the twenty-first century, we behaved like we were still in the Middle

Ages. Our women were not allowed to step out of their houses and not allowed an education. Their only purpose was to serve the men. We were not allowed to drink or listen to western music. Partying is banned. The things which were considered normal in other countries were illegal in Abi and punishable by death.

But we were allowed to do everything elsewhere. So, I traveled the world in the guise of business and engaged in activities that were illegal in my country. I gambled in casinos, had sex with prostitutes, drank all night, took drugs, and danced to western music with my friends. My favorite hobby when I travel abroad is to abduct the girls who I find pretty and ravish them till I was satisfied. I had several thugs under my payroll to kidnap the girls. My prey for the night can be anyone from the girls in school dress returning to their homes to the women walking with their children. If they fall into my category, I ensure that they satisfy me or die a miserable death.

I also had a secret import/export business known only to a few and our products were young girls and boys from all corners of the globe. My clients were the rich and powerful from many countries so no one could touch me.

I was waiting for the girls which I had pointed to my underlings an hour ago in a luxurious bedroom with a glass of scotch when the wind blew open the French windows. I stepped onto the balcony. The last thing I remembered was the icy rain falling on my face.

The bus reached its destination and people started getting off the bus. When I was about to step down, a police woman ran towards me.

You are under arrest for dressing obscenely and seducing other men. She shouted.

I was handcuffed and taken to the police jeep despite the angry protests of Momed. He waved at me sadly as I was taken to the station. In an hour I stood before the female judge with a white wig on her head.

For creating a public nuisance, dressing inappropriately, and involving in sedition is against our beliefs and country. I sentence you to receive 20 lashes by the barbed whip. The judge declared without bothering to listen to my appeal.

I pleaded to the female judge.

Sir, please spare me. I am a foreigner and ignorant of your customs. Please take pity on me.

The Judge looked at me sarcastically.

But you have mentioned that Abi was your birthplace and named Mr.Uddhin as your father to a Mr.Momed.

I bit my lips and shook my head.

Carry out the sentence said the judge.

I stood in line with others mostly male and waited in a dark place. Soon we were led outside and I looked around. It looked like we were in the middle of a miniature Roman amphitheater with raised seats for people around us. The punishments were given in the oval arena in the center. I saw different punishments being carried out in the day. Some were hung by their necks. Some died screaming when the crowd pelted them with stones. Some were killed and mauled by wild animals. The lashing was the kindest punishment of all.

As the lashes tore the skin on my body, I thanked God for being lenient to me. I fainted before the fourth lash landed on my body.

I woke up in a big house and found my father dressed in women's clothes treating my wounds.

Why did you run away he asked in a feminine voice? We provided you with food and clothes, a big roof over your head and many servants to look after your needs.

I opened my mouth to speak when she interrupted.

I know you wanted to study, wear clothes like a man and live like one. But we females are not meant to live like that. We are meant to serve our husbands.

You also denied becoming one of the wives of your dad's friend. I know that he is old enough to be your grandfather but he is the richest man in the city. You would have lived a comfortable life bearing his children and looking after his needs if you had married him. Instead, you rebelled and ran away.

His father pulled the veil and covered his face when someone opened the door.

His mother entered the room semi-nude and walked towards him.

I am afraid that this time you had gone too far. Everyone had heard the news about my slut daughter and the only reason I brought you into this house is to hide you.

After she left, his father bent his head and spoke in his ear.

He plans to kill you in the night so I advise you to run away. I can only offer you some money and a safe passage outside this country. Please be careful he said.

Ulla was on the run again dressed in women's clothes, with a veil covering his face. With the money given by his father, he left the country in a boat hiding from prying eyes. Soon the captain of the ship dropped him in a foreign country. As he roamed the streets, past incidents flooded his mind.

It is the same city.

I used to visit here very often to enjoy my life.

It is the same city.

I came here often to party, to drink, and to take drugs.

It is the same city.

I also prowled the streets searching for my prey and ravished many girls.

It is the same city.

He didn't notice a couple of women following him. Suddenly a cloth that smelled sweet was pressed into his nose and he felt his eyes become heavy. He woke up in a palatial room and found a woman ogling at his naked body with a glass of scotch in her hand.

He looked around and found that it was the same room where he usually sat waiting for the girls.

You are my slave the woman said and took out a giant dildo. Let's hear you scream she said.

Ulla ran to the balcony and jumped from the 20th floor. He heard his skull crack when his head hit the ground and felt no more.

In a secret underground lab, the men in white suits rushed towards the red room.

A man was strapped on the operating table, his body writhing in pain. His head was enclosed in a transparent helmet and various wires were plugged in his nerve centers throughout his body.

A man appeared from the shadows.

Nothing to worry about, the white suits assured him. We can run the simulation again.

Yes, but this time I would like to give him a more interesting scenario. I am sure he will suffer more pain than the previous ones.

Serves him right said the white suits.

As the white suits plugged the machine into his brain, Ulla woke up in a different place.

RAINDROP 9

*All the things one has forgotten
scream for help in dreams.*

Elias Canetti

Love & Amnesia

Prelude

When we are dying, we see our whole life flash through our eyes in the split of a second. I had read it somewhere. It must be true because I saw at least some parts of my life like the movie Memento. The scenes are all jumbled, and it doesn't always make any sense. The scenes keep flipping randomly, but the only thing which does not change is the feeling of raindrops falling on your face.

The everlasting dream

Splat,Splat,Splat

Damn! I cursed loudly listening to the sounds made by my expensive Geox sneakers as I ran trying without success to avoid the puddles on the road.

It started to drizzle when I was chatting with my friends at the coffee shop. The big glass window next to me was riddled with hundreds of raindrops, some standing still, shining brightly while others rolled down to join the others. But I was neither listening to the conversation nor admiring the raindrops. Something else had tantalized me, pulling me away from the present.

My ears concentrated on the commotion a few tables from me in the far corner of the coffee shop, the laughter of children singing merrily. My lips started to move as I joined the children in silent mode fearing that my voice would frighten them away. A deep voice suddenly joined with the children's euphonious symphony which prodded me to turn my head to look at the interloper but my friend's voice brought me back to my senses.

Looking at my friend's frantic motions with her hands, pointing at the watch and her mouth clicking like a dolphin, I realized that I was late for my next session. As I gathered my hand bag, my iPhone, and my scooter's keys, I caught a glimpse of the scene at the back which almost made me to drop my stuff.

Cursing silently, I slipped out of the coffee shop with my heart racing and moved swiftly towards the parking lot as the rain started falling heavily.

I could see that my Honda Activa tilting dangerously and would soon fall which made me run faster when I heard another set of feet splashing on the water-logged road.

Now I realized that my legs were losing the marathon to my heart as the former slowed down it's pace while the latter galloped like a charger in the home stretch.

It didn't take long to realize that I stood still now, completely drenched and shivering like a withered moss, on tenterhooks for the grand finale.

Do you believe in love at first sight?

No

Why?

Because you get attracted, at first sight, a sort of infatuation. Like a fad.

What about Love?

Love is like a tree. At first, you don't know if it is there. Like a seedling deep in the ground, you only know when the first sprouts are visible. That's when you feel butterflies in your stomach.

The more you nurture it, the quicker it grows. It rises from the ground when its roots had penetrated deep enough. That's when you realize that it is serious. Your love grows stronger as the weak stem thickens into a strong bark. It matures into a full-grown tree with branches spreading out and covered with thick foliage of leaves.

Is it not possible for love at first sight?

Not always.

Sometimes it may happen.

Knock,Knock,Knock

I woke up on a comfy sofa and looked around me. At first, it felt that I was in a strange place but soon I realized that I was in my home. It was exactly as I had imagined and dreamed about since childhood. I was in a cozy living room, warmed by the burning wood in the fireplace and I could see the big kitchen through the arched doorway. I must have drunk last night because I was too lethargic to move my body. I forced myself to stand and slowly my body responded to my command. I moved slowly to the kitchen and watched the beautiful walnut cabinets arranged in an L shape with a matching island table in the center. Fresh herbs grew in beautiful pots over the island table and the window sills.

It was my dream kitchen as I loved to cook.

I heard my phone ring. I recognized who it was by my favorite ringtone. It was my husband calling me. I answered the phone.

Do you remember the first time we met?

He had asked me the same question many times in the past but I could not recollect even when I wracked my brains.

I heard thunder in the distance. It was about to rain and I saw Akash, my 3-year-old boy, and Dakshi, my 6-year-old girl playing in the garden from the window in the kitchen. I opened the large patio doors and stepped barefoot in the grass.

Come children, I shouted. It's time to go inside.

They looked at me and smiled.

I stood there looking at my beautiful kids, playing innocently with our little pup. Sometimes it is tough being a mother, really tough. You want your kids to listen to you at the same time cannot bear to see the disappointment in their faces. I saw the lightning flash in the sky and the wall of rain moving towards us.

The first raindrops fell on my face and seemed to seep through my skin.

Come children, I said and took their hands. Let's go inside.

Grabbing their hands tightly I ran towards the house.

Why are you running, mom asked my teenaged girl and let go of my hands. I am old enough to walk alone, she said.

I lost my directions for a second.

I looked at my college-going girl and wondered how she had transformed into this beautiful girl from a pixyish-looking toothless baby. I accompanied her to the bus stop since it was her first day of college against her wishes.

Some teenagers were waiting at the bus stop. Maybe they went to the same college as my daughter. My daughter was very shy and slow at making friends. Someone had to give her a boost. The others were checking her out and my girl tried hard not to look at them growing embarrassed by the second.

I looked at the corner of my eye and saw that she was twirling her hair. She was also peeking at a handsome boy. She was blooming into a young woman.

Come with me I said.

Why?

Let's chat with those youngsters over there, maybe they go to your college.

No mom, she said and pulled my hand.

As I walked towards them with my girl pulling my hand, I felt a soft breeze on my face, followed by raindrops.

I closed my eyes.

I squeezed my girl's hands tightly.

I felt my hand being squeezed.

I want you to be brave said a voice.

I opened my eyes and the bright lights made me squint.

It's going to be ok said, my husband. I am with you and it would be over in a few seconds.

Do you remember the first time we met?

I was lying on a stretcher moving forward fast and my husband's head looked over me, He squeezed my hands again as I looked at my bloated tummy. The feeling of terror gripped me as I realized that I was taken to the labor ward. I was pregnant and soon I would be a mother. I would soon be looking into my baby's face and feel her tender body grasping me. I would soon feel the baby's lips sucking my breast.

When the stretcher was about to enter the labor ward, my husband let go of my hand and spoke. Please bring back an angel. I tried to grasp his hands, but couldn't as I was wheeled into the room. I saw the lights in the ceiling move rapidly and suddenly felt light-headed.

Don't squint your eyes said, someone. Again, shouted the voice.

It took a few seconds for my eyes to adjust to the bright lights that were focused on me and I heard the click sounds of a camera taking pictures

A man with a DSLR camera was looking at me with frustration. He was one of my closest friends from high school.

Sakshi, he cried, do you want to look beautiful in the pictures because if you do, stop squinting your bloody eyes. Adhav bro, tell her to focus.

Come on girl said a familiar voice clutching my hands. Do you want me to look cuter than you in our marriage album? I think your friend will soon burst with anger, so try to do as he says.

I was wearing a beautiful red colored lehenga and my husband was wearing a brown blazer with red accents. He looked very handsome with his face glowing with happiness.

He bent down and whispered in my ears.

Do you remember the first time we met?

We married that morning in the registrar's office, surrounded by our friends, and after nine hours was posing for group photos in our reception. I kept searching for my parents in the crowd but couldn't find them.

Sakshi, my friend cried. Can you please focus?

After enduring the long session trying to smile at the camera with a deep longing to see my parents and the fear of the future, I followed my husband to the dining room to take a rest and regain our energy. We sat before the long steel tables covered with paper rolls and banana leaves filled with various kinds of foods. I felt my stomach groan with hunger but somehow didn't feel like touching the leaf. I could only stare at the food when Adhav leaned closer to my ears.

I can understand that you were expecting your parents he whispered. I will be incredibly happy to see their faces and get their blessings. Don't lose hope even if they didn't come, today and I assure you that I will make things right.

Tears rolled down my cheeks as I tried to hide from others by putting my head on his shoulders. He grasped my shoulder tightly as if to say that he would be there as my guardian angel, protecting me like my father and caring for me like my mother.

My parents didn't come that day. They didn't like Adhav because of many reasons. He was an orphan and grew under the care of the sisters. He was a social worker and didn't have a high-paying job. He was not intelligent and sophisticated.

My parents saw only his bank balance, his prospects of getting a job in the US, and his unknown pedigree. I saw his good nature, his kindness towards others, his honesty, and his innocence. Moreover, his love was pure, so pure that it illuminated my soul. I wished that my parents would at least glimpse at the real him, but they did not. I packed my things and moved out of my parent's house. I didn't tell them that I was carrying his child.

Most of the well-wishers had left and a few of our friends were there helping to settle the bills. It began to rain as we ran to the car, his hands clutching my hands tightly so that I would not get lost. As I tried to get inside the car, my legs slipped on the wet ground before I bumped my head hard on the car's roof. My head started to spin and I saw Adhav's figure passing my vision repeatedly as if I was watching him from a carousel ride.

Happiness caused by Agony

Mrs. Sakshi, I heard a voice calling in the distance, Are you alright.

A doctor was preening my eyes open and was checking them with a pencil light. I lay on the table with my legs wide open and was embarrassed to see a couple of heads examining them. And suddenly I felt excruciating pain as I went into labor.

Take a deep breath and push. I heard the voices repeating the sentence repeatedly.

I did as they asked. I pushed harder. I huffed and I puffed like the big bad wolf till I ran out of breath. But the voices kept on urging me to push. At first, nothing happened, but soon I felt something move in my belly.

I can see the head shouted the head looking between my legs.

Now the baby has started to come out, the head was talking to me.

Now push harder the voice commanded.

I had been pushing for ages with all my strength.

I can't do it. I shouted back and lay on the bed crying.

Calm down, Mrs. Sakshi. Bear the pain for a few more minutes. I want you to push one last time. Take a deep breath.

I gripped tightly to someone and gathering whatever strength left in me, I pushed harder than ever. It didn't matter if I died after pushing my baby out. In those few minutes, I felt every emotion that had been given a name by humans.

As the baby slipped out, I felt a sensation of relief and happiness. I saw my baby in the hands of the doctor. It's a beautiful girl, I heard him saying. I looked at her tiny eyes looking at me. I raised my hands to hold my baby but slipped into unconsciousness.

I woke up from reality

I woke up to the voices of many people shouting simultaneously and saw many heads looking at me when my vision cleared. I felt a throbbing pain in my head and couldn't feel my body.

I think she is alive said, someone.

I thought she was a goner said another.

Move out of my way said a voice louder than others as I saw him. His face stood out clearly amongst a hundred blurred faces as I was lifted from the ground and placed on a bed inside an ambulance. It was the same face, the one from my dreams.

Adhav, I screamed and raised my hands towards him. Take care of our kids.

My eyes grew heavy and the scene vanished.

Are dreams really memories?

I realized that I was in a hospital when I woke up. I didn't know how long I was out and remembered that I was on the way to the school to pick my children. Maybe I met with an accident. Anyway, I didn't feel any pain but felt a dull throb in my head as if someone was pounding my brain.

Did I see my husband watching me from a distance as I was taken to the ambulance? Then it must have been him, I concluded who had brought me here.

A nurse entered the room with a file in her hand and was checking the readings on the monitor when I called her.

Sister

The one word startled her so much that she dropped her file and looked at me with fear.

The fear in her face turned into bewilderment and then to happiness.

Madam, you are finally awake. I will fetch the doctor.

She ran away before I could utter another word.

I wanted to see my husband and waited anxiously to see his figure burst through the doors. The doors were pushed open but saw only my parents rushing towards me. I was in their tight embrace and was soothed by their kind words. I realized that I had last seen them 10 years before. My eyes welled up when my memories about my parents that I had buried deep in my heart resurfaced when they hugged me.

I miss you, mom, and dad. How did you know that I met with an accident? Did you meet my husband? You had forgotten about me for the last ten years but I had shown your picture to my children. If they were here, they would have recognized you as their grandparents.

It was my parent's turn to look at me with fear.

What is it, dad? I asked. What is it, mom?

It's alright dear, you have not recovered fully. The doctors had warned us about your condition. Don't overwork your brain and take some rest said, my mom.

It's alright mom. I feel fine moreover I must pick my children from school and can you tell me the time?

My mother looked at me in shock.

What is the time, dad?

It's 4 P.M. said my dad after looking at his watch.

Dammit, I am late. I had to pick them at 3.30 P.M. Dad, can you pick them from the Little Angels School, please.

I will try; he blurted and left the room followed by my mother.

The nurse was still looking at me like I was crazy.

Can you remove these things from sticking in my body?

Sorry, I can't without the approval of the doctor she replied.

Do you have children? I asked her casually.

Yes, she said. A boy and a girl

Me too, I said with a smile.

God bless you my child she said and scampered from the room.

The chief doctor came with two doctors and he examined me.

My parents were summoned inside.

She looks fine and all her functions are normal. Still, she must be under observation and you can take her home within two or three days said the chief doctor.

There is a problem doctor. It was my father who interrupted him.

The chief doctor looked at him for an explanation when I requested the doctor to discharge me sooner since my children would miss me.

I see said the chief doctor and nodded at my dad.

Sometimes a person suffers from acute stress disorder after recovering from a major injury to the head and your daughter is also experiencing such trauma but it is treatable with time. I recommend a daily sit-in with a good psychologist.

Dad, I called him. Where is my husband? Could you please ask him to pick the children? I insisted.

Could you please stop talking about picking the children?

I couldn't believe what I was hearing.

Why dad?

I can't explain everything now. The doctors have given explicit instructions to not give any details because they feel that it will overwhelm your brain. So, I have no other choice. Please stop asking any more questions.

My father spoke with anger and left.

I knew something was wrong and my parents were trying to hide something. It had everything to do with them and maybe they were trying to isolate me from my husband and children. It was 9.00 A.M. today morning when I started from my house, driving my scooter to purchase groceries at the local department and I would have met with the accident on the way. It was 4.00 P.M. now so seven hours had passed between the accident and the present.

I couldn't believe that my husband hadn't visited me till now. Where is he? I wondered.

I begged my mom to call my husband.

I didn't know that I had started to scream

A team of nurses entered the room and inserted something in my hand. I once again slipped into my dreamland.

I was on the way to Adhav's room in a mansion near the market. I could not forget the incidents that happened earlier that day, I had taken him to meet my parents, but they had insulted him with very harsh words that made me cringe. He listened to them very calmly and without replying to a single word he left. I didn't find him in the places he usually frequented and thought of going to his room. Despite his warnings not to visit his place of dwelling as it was habituated by other lonely unmarried people, I was now climbing the stairs of the mansion. I walked with a straight face knowing that a thousand eyes were dissecting my body. He was not in his room and no one knew where he had gone.

I hoped that he would come to see me in the next few days but he never did. I passed my days thinking about him and the nights dreaming about him.

I was daydreaming as usual when my mother's voice interrupted.

It's raining cats and dogs outside. Look at the lightning flash.

A clap of thunder crashed loudly that made my mother jump.

I have never seen such heavy rainfall in my life, my mother said. She said that every time it rained.

Now when did I see such rain before, I thought.

Burning in the dark

A voice answered; do you remember the first time we met?

Adhav and I were running towards a hut to escape from the rain. It didn't matter as we were both drenched. I had accompanied him to volunteer for a medical camp in a tiny village. I had not expected the rain as I wore a simple white churidar and it stuck to my body exposing a lot of skin.

The hut was empty and dark but I could feel his eyes probing my body. I wanted him to look at me. I felt a mixture of fear and anxiety: fear because of what would happen next and anxiety of whether it would not happen. I felt his presence remarkably close to me and waited for his next move.

I found a light he said as he lit a candle from the far side of the room and saw his innocent face illuminated by the light.

It was all in my imagination. What a naughty girl you are? I chided myself.

He came towards me and the light would soon expose my wet body. Before he could step closer, I ran and hugged him tightly.

Once again darkness filled the hut when the candle slipped from his hands and fell. Our eyes couldn't see each other but our hands did as we let it roam freely. We made love till the sun shone brightly and daylight filled the hut.

I opened my eyes and saw my clothes lay scattered on the floor. But I could not find him. I stood up listening to the cacophony of voices getting louder by the second. Where was I?

As I looked outside the window, the brightness intensified. My eyes soon adjusted to the light and I found myself in a long hallway of a hospital. I instinctively covered my body with my hands but found that I was wearing a blue hospital dress. People walked past me without another glance. Soon there was a disturbance when I saw some of the nurses running towards me.

Where are you going? You are not supposed to wander without supervision. Please come back without making a fuss. I heard someone say as they surrounded me.

They led me down the hallway and found from the signboard that I was being taken to the psychiatry ward. As I was made to lie on the bed in a small room, I screamed at the top of my voice demanding them to release me.

Where is my husband, I shouted. I want to see my children. I know that my parents had paid you a lot of money to keep me away from my family. Please can't you understand the feelings of a mother yearning for her children?

I heard someone giggle and I lashed at her face. I fought hard with others who tried to subdue me at the same time screaming and cursing them with obscene words.

Your husband is dead, I heard someone say between the commotions.

What did you say? I asked the face who uttered those terrible words. Her face was in great pain and bloody.

I said that your husband is dead and so are your children. It's now your turn to die, bitch.

I kicked out at them with all my strength.

You liars, I cried. Murderers and cutthroats. You lying whores and bastards.

I didn't know how long I shouted but soon fell asleep after a needle pricked into my skin.

It was a whirlpool of dreams where the memories tormented the dreamer with agony and pleasure, where the dreamer relives his most memorable moments repeatedly.

I was hugging my girl on her first birthday, our faces covered with cream, and my husband dressed as a clown.

The scene changed and I was begging my parents to approve the marriage.

Then I was shopping with my girl at a big sari showroom and looked at my husband and son waiting with sullen faces near the counter.

I was slapped for the first time by my dad and looked at my mother for support but her face showed that I should not expect any.

We were talking on our first night, me and my husband in the same hut where we first made love.

I packed my bags and left the house in the middle of the night, filled with terror.

I was with my husband and children, on a vacation in a snowy place and eating hot momos and sipping hot tea.

I was driving my scooter and saw the speeding lorry on the opposite side swerve. I remembered the terrible crash and my flight in the air towards a lamp post. The crunching noise of my skull cracking echoed repeatedly in my ears.

When I regained consciousness, I saw many faces watching me. My parents were one of the faces and I could recognize some nurses and doctors.

I heard the doctors explaining that my situation had turned serious and was suggesting a different treatment.

I decided to make a run for it. I waited till I was fully awake and before anyone could react, I ran out of the room. I heard the noises of a dozen people shouting together and ran towards the entrance. Fortunately, I saw a police officer and ran towards him.

Please save me I shouted at the top of my voice. They are keeping me forcefully and I want to return to my husband and children.

Hi Sakshi, the officer said. Don't you remember me? I am Arjun.

Yes, I know you. How can I forget one of my closest friends since high school?

What happened to you? Your parents told me that you had gone abroad for higher studies but instead, you are wandering in a hospital like a mad person.

My parents are liars, I shouted. They have been keeping me captive in this hospital by giving them a lot of money just because I was in love with a person they didn't approve of.

Arjun saw the nurses rushing towards them.

I warn you not to come near her. If you do, you will feel my knuckles cracking your jaws. Now, where are her parents?

I hid behind him when I saw my mother and father approaching.

Hi Arjun, we can explain everything, they said.

Why did you lie that you had sent her abroad, uncle? Arjun shouted back.

My father turned towards me. Why were you running away, he asked me?

To find my husband and children who are probably in great danger because of you. You had instructed one of the nurses to lie that they were dead but I didn't believe her.

What are you talking about, Sakshi? Who is your husband?

Arjun gripped my shoulders and asked me.

Don't you remember him? You were the one taking pictures during our reception. Don't you remember Adhav? I asked him pleadingly.

He turned to my parents and apologized.

I am sorry to intrude without clarifying and I would like to offer any help within my power he said.

Take care Sakshi, he told me and left.

I kept on screaming begging him to rescue me until my voice turned hoarse.

Four years later

I was working in a software company and still trying to accept the truth that I had never been married and was still a virgin. I met with a serious accident when I was returning home after partying with my friends. The blow to my head was profoundly serious so my body shut itself and my brain automatically went into coma mode.

Everything was like a dream. No. Everything was a dream. But it was so real. The pleasure when we made love, the excruciating pain of delivering a child, the happiness of caring for my children and my husband were so real.

But the doctors explained that the brain was the most complicated organ in the human body and still we had a lot to learn about its mysteries.

I was walking with my colleagues towards the coffee shop where we were regulars. On the way, I saw some children explaining traffic rules to a group of motorists standing pathetically. The white-dressed police officer was insisting the rule-breakers listen to the children's speech.

We watched the funny scene till the end when the motorists were let off with a warning and walked to the coffee shop. A man in a white t-shirt and blue jeans was taking the children inside the coffee shop. I couldn't see his face but he looked familiar.

We sat in our usual seats in the usually silent coffee shop when the silence was broken by a loud cheer from the children. The man was entertaining them with his antics. I still couldn't see his face.

After we finished our drinks, we dispersed. I was walking towards the place where I had parked my scooter when a voice called from behind.

Do you believe in love at first sight?

Raindrops will always carry their dreams and hopes with them, no matter where they go

Anthony T Hincks

The End

www.ingramcontent.com/pod-product-compliance
Lightning Source LLC
LaVergne TN
LVHW041842070526
838199LV00045BA/1400